The
Great Train Robbery
of Monroe County

J.L. Fredrick

Lovstad Publishing
Poynette, Wisconsin

First Edition

ISBN-13: 978-0615746630

Printed in the United States of America

For Rachel and Nancy

Other Titles By J.L. Fredrick

Mad City Bust
September Ten
Aftermath
Cursed by the Wind
Another Shade of Gray
Across the Dead Line
The Other End of the Tunnel

Non-Fiction

Rivers, Roads, & Rails

The GREAT TRAIN ROBBERY of MONROE COUNTY

Chapter 1

Mixed emotions raced through Jackson Evans as he stepped onto the boarding platform at the railroad depot. He'd never been on a train; he'd never set foot outside of his hometown, other than climbing the bluffs overlooking the Mississippi River. He was just seventeen years old, and although he was quite physically fit, he knew he looked more the part of a choirboy than a lumberjack. But he was determined. Stepping onto the train was his first step on the journey to his new adventure.

As he made his way toward an empty seat at the middle of the car, he glanced down at the satchel in his grip that contained wool socks, long johns, wool shirt and trousers, scarf and deerskin mittens with wool liners... all the things that would help keep him warm out in the woods this winter. He had seen the advertisement in the *La Crosse Democrat* by a man named Abernathy who was willing to hire several men to clear trees from his farmland near West Salem. It wasn't like going into the pineries of the far north, as so many of the men folk in La Crosse did every winter—just as his father would travel up the Mississippi by steamer to Read's Landing at the mouth of the Chippewa, and then up that river to Eau Claire—*Sawdust City*—to join a crew that would head yet farther north into the great pine forest to fell hundreds of thousands of trees, and not return until spring.

But Jackson would travel only about fifteen miles—one

station stop away on the *Chicago, Milwaukee & St. Paul.* He even promised his mother he would be home for Christmas, and by then he would have made enough money to buy presents for her and his two little brothers... something he had never done before.

He was still daydreaming about all the wonderful things that were about to change his life when he heard the faint ring of the bell on the engine, and then the shrill scream of the whistle, and then he felt the jerk as the train started to slowly move forward. He watched through the window next to his seat as the La Crosse Depot slid away and disappeared, along with all the other familiar surroundings he had grown up with. Within minutes the city was out of sight, and Jackson was staring at the ever changing landscape he had only heard about from other travelers. What would he do in another town where he'd never been? How would he find his way in a strange place?

Several miles of hills, trees, and river valley had marched past his window when the gentleman sitting next to him must have recognized the doubt in Jackson's eyes. He probably noticed that tiny element of fear that Jackson was so desperately trying to hide. He offered his right hand and said, "I'm Theodore... going to Chicago. How far you going?"

Jackson broke his gaze out the window to look at the man's friendly smile, and then accepted the handshake. "Jackson," he said, mimicking Theodore's words. "Just to the next stop... West Salem."

"Oh," Theodore replied, as if he were disappointed. "So I won't have the pleasure of your company but for a few more minutes."

"Yeah. I guess so. I'm applying for a job there."

Although this encounter with a perfect stranger would last only a brief time, the next few minutes would provide a measure of confidence for Jackson that would prevent him from losing his nerve.

"Never traveled much, eh?" Theodore asked.

"No, sir."

"Well, don't you worry none. I remember when I first started traveling. It was mostly stagecoach and riverboats then. Took this job that required a lot of traveling... Chicago, St. Louis, New York, all over. Guess I was a little scared, too, at first."

Jackson eased out a little sigh. "But you got over it?"

"Oh, sure. I discovered that no matter where I went in this grand country, I could always find a friend, somehow, just as I did not two minutes ago."

Jackson smiled. "But we'll never see each other again... ever."

"Doesn't matter. I still made a friend, Jackson. And if we don't ever meet again, we won't ever quarrel about anything, and if we never quarrel, that means we'll always be friends."

Pondering that thought for a few moments, Jackson decided that Theodore possessed a pretty good philosophy— one that he would make his own, too. "So, do you get lonely traveling alone all the time?"

"Sure. But it never lasts too long. I just think about the friends I've met, and how glad I'll be to see them again some day. And then the loneliness goes away."

"Do you ever get lost when you're in a strange place?"

"Shucks, yes. In fact, sometimes I enjoy getting lost."

"You do? Why?"

"Because, then I have to talk to somebody to help me

5

find my way, and what d'ya know? I've made another friend."

"I'm kinda worried, though, about getting homesick."

Theodore looked sincerely into Jackson's eyes and patted his shoulder. "Don't worry, Jackson. A handsome young boy like you will make so many friends, you won't have time to be homesick."

Just then they heard the long whistle from the engine. The next stop—Jackson's stop—was just minutes away. He would soon step off the train into a new town, and into a new life. He offered his hand to Theodore. "Good-bye, Theodore. Have a good trip to Chicago... and thank you for the good advice. Maybe we'll meet again some day." He picked up the satchel from the floor and trudged to the front of the car where the Conductor was calling for passengers who were to disembark at West Salem.

Chapter 2

J ackson didn't know what to expect at this place. After living his whole life, so far, in the magnificent beauty of the Upper Mississippi River Valley, he was afraid anything else might seem dull. But to his pleasant surprise, there in the La Crosse River Valley, the little river, hills, trees and the remains of the wilderness gathered in such a way to make him feel as though he might have discovered paradise. He could easily understand why the settlers who came here decided to stay. There seemed to be a breath of success in the air as if everything had turned out just the way it was planned.

The village of West Salem lay in the wide valley of the La Crosse River. Jackson couldn't help but admire the pleasantness that seemed to abound. The streets were adorned with numerous shade trees, although at this time of year most had shed their foliage, or were still clinging to a few remnants of crimson, gold and brown. He could only imagine the greenery that summer would bring.

With two railroads—the *Milwaukee & St. Paul*, and the *Chicago & North Western*—this was a busy little town that had become the major shipping point of the territory. This was late October, the beginning of the busiest shipping season; over the next few months, nearly 200 carloads of livestock would be shipped from here to markets in Milwaukee and Chicago, not to mention the countless carloads of wheat and corn. It meant that the streets of West Salem would be constantly alive with farmers' teams and wagons, and with herds of cattle, sheep and hogs on the hoof,

7

destined for the stockyards just down the road from the passenger and freight depot.

Just up Leonard Street from the depot, the heart of downtown West Salem began with stores and shops, eateries and hotels. Jackson gazed at the sight, and then pulled out his pocket watch. It was 11:30. The advertisement had stated that Mr. Abernathy would receive applications in front of the hotel from noon to one o'clock on Thursday. He had more than enough time to walk the three blocks to the City Hotel at the corner of Leonard and Main, but it wouldn't hurt to be a little early.

Jackson soon realized that his concerns about finding his way, or getting lost had been rather foolish; this town was quite small in comparison with La Crosse—merely a few blocks in any direction. He sensed eyes following him, looking him over as he strode toward the hotel, yet when he scanned the faces on the street, hardly anyone seemed to notice him at all.

With plenty of time to reach his destination, he ducked into the Haberdashery on his way; the sign painted on the front window said Victor Johnson: proprietor. Jackson browsed a while among the many shirts, coats, hats, socks— everything a man could possibly need in the way of clothing—and then he politely asked the man behind the counter, who he assumed was Mr. Johnson, "Do you have any handkerchiefs? I seem to have lost mine."

"Certainly," the man replied. He opened a drawer behind the counter, pulled out several and laid them neatly in a row on the counter for Jackson to inspect.

"How much are they?" the boy asked.

"Ten cents each. But if you'd prefer, I have some very

nice silk handkerchiefs for twenty-five cents."

"Oh, no. These will do," Jackson said. "I'll take two of these." He pointed to a white one, and a red one with little white dots. He paid the clerk and stuffed the new handkerchiefs into his satchel. As he left through the front door, the clerk smiled and thanked him and invited him to return when he needed anything else.

When he passed a General Store just up the street, he felt the urge for gum drops and went inside.

"Would there be anything else you need?" the clerk asked as he exchanged the bag of candy for Jackson's nickel.

"Well, I will need a place to stay," Jackson said rather shyly. "Do happen you know where I might find a room? I'm seeing a man about a job this afternoon."

The tall skinny fellow behind the counter turned to another man who was negotiating the price of potatoes with another customer. "Hey, Ted? Does Mrs. Jorgenson have any rooms available now?"

Ted had apparently reached an agreement with his customer, grinned, and sauntered over to Jackson. "Are you the one looking for a room?"

"Yes, sir. I am."

"Well, you can talk to Millicent Jorgenson. Her boarding house is at the west end of Franklin Street. It's a big white, two-story house with a nice green hedge around it." While he talked, he was jotting the name on a small pad of paper with the pencil he pulled from behind his ear. "A young gentleman who lived there just got married, and he moved to another town." He handed the slip of paper to Jackson. "Mrs. Jorgenson is a nice lady. She keeps a clean house, and she's a very good cook."

"Thank you, Ted. Maybe I'll see her this afternoon." Jackson stuffed his bag of gum drops into his satchel, the slip of paper into his pocket, and headed out the door feeling quite pleased with finding friendly, helpful people in this new, unfamiliar town. He thought about what Theodore on the train had told him, and he realized that he had already made two new friends.

At the corner of Main and Leonard Streets, Jackson stood in front of the North Star Saloon where three farmers were discussing how they would help each other herd their cattle to the railroad stockyard. He listened for a while and determined that none of these men were Mr. Abernathy. But he did see a man wearing a splendid leather jacket with fur collar and cuffs across the street in front of the hotel. A fine-looking hat that perfectly matched his leather coat covered most of his gray hair, and an almost white mustache and nicely-trimmed beard adorned his weathered face. He held some papers in his hand, and he looked like a wealthy land owner. Jackson started walking toward him.

Just as he reached the other side of the street he saw the leather jacketed man greet and shake hands with another younger man who apparently was looking for work, too. "Charlie McCoy," Jackson heard the man announce his name. Jackson sidestepped a few paces as not to interfere with the conversation already started. But he remained close to insure he would be the next one Mr. Abernathy would greet.

When he had finished with McCoy, Mr. Abernathy turned to Jackson. He had noticed him standing there as if waiting his turn. For a moment he studied Jackson's broad shoulders and strong arms, and then he offered his right hand. "Edwin Abernathy," he said. "And you are...?"

"Jackson Evans. I saw your advertisement in the newspaper. I came from La Crosse on the train this morning."

"Well, Jackson, I have a couple hundred acres of land up the valley that needs a few trees cleared. It'd make good cropland if it weren't for those darn trees."

Jackson just nodded and listened.

"I need a few good men to cut those trees and clear the brush. Think you can handle that kind of work?"

"Yes, sir. My father goes to the north woods on the Chippewa every winter. I've learned a lot about cutting trees from him."

"Well, Jackson," Abernathy said, rubbing his chin. "You look a little young..."

Jackson's forehead wrinkled with a frown and his eyes narrowed with disappointment. He'd come all this way just to get rejected for the job he really wanted.

"But you look healthy and strong, and I'll hire you on. Pay is twenty-five dollars a month. You can have every Saturday and Sunday off. Only problem is... I don't have a bunkhouse yet."

Jackson found a grin with his sigh of relief. "That's okay, Mr. Abernathy. I'll find someplace to stay here in town. Ted at the General Store told me about a place."

"Okay," Abernathy said. "Here's a map to show you how to get to my place." He handed Jackson a white sheet of paper. "It's only about a mile. Just follow the road out of town at the end of Jefferson Street."

Jackson briefly studied the hand-drawn map and then pointed toward the east. "It's that way out of town?"

"Yep. I'll pair you up with McCoy—that other fellow that

11

just left. Come out to my place about ten o'clock on Monday."

With wings on his heels and a song in his heart, Jackson strolled down Leonard Street. This was the best feeling of satisfaction he had ever experienced. In just a few days he would be a wage earner, and of that he was proud.

He looked up just in time to see the sign that said "Franklin Street." He took out the little slip of paper Ted at the General Store had given him. It said: *Millicent Jorgenson. Franklin Street. Hedge.*

The sun was still high and bright in the western sky, but the west wind had a chilly autumn bite. He turned up the collar of his wool shirt, stuffed the paper back into his pocket, started down Franklin Street, and quietly whistled Yankee Doodle. It was the only tune that came to mind.

Chapter 3

Jackson found Mrs. Jorgenson's boarding house on the west edge of town at the end of Franklin Street. It was a large two-story frame house with painted shutters on all the windows, and a roofed porch that stretched the full front length of the house.

A cedar hedge that was little more than waist high encircled the entire yard around the house except for an opening six feet wide at the front, and another just like it at the rear. Large flat rocks formed a walkway all the way from the street, through the hedge opening and to the front entrance.

Jackson noticed how green the hedge looked, compared to all the rusty, drab brown of the autumn season.

Millicent Jorgenson stood on the front porch as if she had been expecting him. Tall and sturdy, Millicent appeared well-adapted to frontier life, but she had that gentle motherly smile, and gentle blue eyes that seemed to welcome Jackson into her home and into her heart without speaking a single word.

He had dropped his satchel at his feet to dig the little slip of paper from his pocket, but he hadn't looked at it because he easily remembered the woman's name. And because this was the only house at the end of the street with a nice, green hedge, he already knew he had found the right place.

"Are you Mrs. Jorgenson?" he asked, a little shyness

guarding his voice.

"Ya, sure, I am," the woman replied before Jackson had finished speaking her name. "I betcha you're here about da room."

He was just a little stunned at first that this woman knew the nature of his call without him announcing his purpose. He wanted to ask her if she was a fortune-teller, or maybe a witch of some sort, but his sense of good manners took charge. "How did you know?"

She smiled and gave a little chuckle. "I run a boarding house, and I have rooms to rent. It's not suppertime yet, so I know you're not here to eat. You must be looking for a room."

That all made perfect sense to Jackson, now that he thought about it. "Well, yeah, I guess I am."

By then she had stepped off the porch, approached the handsome young lad and put her arm across his shoulders. "Vell, you come right in and have a look... it's a very nice room."

Jackson picked up his satchel and allowed the woman to guide him up the porch steps and through the front door. Just inside she turned him to the right toward a staircase, and then stepped ahead of him to lead the way to the second floor.

Jackson liked the woman already. In this very short time, he had already become fond of her Scandinavian accent... Norwegian or Swedish, he wasn't certain. She made him feel like they had been friends all their lives, yet they had just met.

"How much is the room?" he asked as they climbed the stairs. He desperately hoped the rent would be within his means.

At the top of the stairs, Millicent stopped as if to catch her breath, turned toward Jackson and smiled. "Two dollars a veek for da room, and if you vant meals, vell, dat's another two dollars a veek." Then she led him down a narrow hallway past several closed doors while he figured in his head his monthly expenditure. Sixteen dollars a month seemed reasonable for a warm bed to sleep in under a roof and all his meals. If the food was as good as Mrs. Jorgenson was friendly, then he had struck a bonanza. He'd even have nine dollars a month left over.

They came to an open door on the left where she motioned him to enter. The room wasn't large, but when he was inside, Jackson realized it must be at the end of the house, as there were windows on two adjacent walls, providing an abundance of sunlight. During the cold winter months not far ahead, sun through a southern exposure window could be a good thing. And during the warmer summer, those open windows would provide a satisfying cool breeze.

Simply furnished with a bed, small bureau, chair, wash basin and water pitcher, and several hooks on the wall for hanging extra clothes, Jackson thought the room was exquisite—much better than he had hoped for. It was nearly as good as the room he had left behind in La Crosse, and he didn't have to share this one with his little brothers.

The excitement of his new adventure was overwhelming. "This'll do very nicely," he said with enthusiasm bubbling out. "I will start working for Mr. Abernathy next Monday. When can I move in?"

"Vell," Millicent said, smiling at the boy's jubilation.

"You've got your bag in hand, and you're here, so I guess you already did."

Jackson tossed his satchel on the bed to make it official.

"But I s'pose I should at least know your name," Millicent said as she turned toward the open door.

"Jackson. Jackson Evans."

"Okay, Jackson Evans. Rent's due every Saturday. Today is Thursday, so I von't charge you for the rest of dis veek... okay?" She gave Jackson a wink. "Breakfast is at six every morning in the dining room downstairs, and supper's at six every night." With that Mrs. Jorgenson stepped out into the hallway. As an afterthought she said, "Key's in the door... don't lose it." And then she was out of sight.

Jackson closed *his* door, turned the key, just to make sure the lock worked, and flopped down on the bed. Now it really was official.

Chapter 4

He'd been up since 5 AM that morning getting ready for this, and he hadn't slept much because of anxious anticipation. So it wasn't difficult for him to drift off into a little nap. When he awoke, it took a few minutes for the grogginess to wear off and to clear his thoughts about the new and unfamiliar surroundings. Hunger growled in his gut; he looked at his pocket watch and realized that it was two hours until supper. The only way to keep his mind off the hunger was to keep himself busy until 6 o'clock.

Only ten minutes had passed by the time he had put away his warm clothes in the bureau drawers. He hung an extra heavy wool shirt on one of the wall hooks, just for the sake of making the room feel a little more lived-in with it there. Then he slid the empty satchel under the bed and decided there was nothing better to do than to go for a walk around town to occupy his time until supper.

At the bottom of the stairs, he met Mrs. Jorgenson carrying a mug of coffee toward the front door. She smiled and went out onto the porch, and Jackson followed.

"Jacob!" she called out. But the scruffy-looking character leaned back in a chair just continued to snore loudly.

"Jackson," Mrs. Jorgenson said. "Would you like this coffee? Doesn't look like he's going to wake up just yet."

Jackson was willing to take anything, at that point, that might fill some of the void in his stomach. "Sure," he said as he took the mug. "Who's that?" He eyed the man in the chair.

"That's Jacob. He lives here and I feed him. He takes care of my chickens and cows, but mostly he hunts and brings in meat for our table. There's a big fat goose roasting in the oven right now for supper."

Jackson sipped the coffee. Just the thought of a roasting goose made his stomach growl even louder.

"You're going to be here for supper, aren't you?" Mrs. Jorgenson asked.

"Oh, sure," Jackson replied. "I'm looking forward to it, Mrs. Jorgenson."

"Why don't you just call me Millie? That's what everybody here calls me."

After Millie had returned into the house to look after the roasting goose, Jackson remained on the porch just long enough to finish the coffee. He set the empty mug on a little table next to the snoring Jacob and then started out on the walk. He still had an hour to kill.

He had committed Abernathy's map to memory, and he thought he would walk out past the railroad depot to where the road led away from town. Just after he turned the corner and headed south on Leonard Street, another young fellow trotted his horse alongside Jackson, and then just kept an even pace with him. He couldn't help notice the holstered sidearm at the rider's waist, and he wondered if he had now encountered his first adversary on this new adventure. He felt a thumping in his chest as he picked up the pace. What did this weapon-bearing hoodlum want of him? Entertaining the thought of trying to make a run for the depot or back to the boarding house, he abruptly realized that there was no chance of escaping two blocks on foot against a rider on horseback.

"Hey, what's your hurry?" the rider finally said. There was no hostility in the voice; Jackson thought it even sounded cheery and inviting, so he slowed his pace and stopped. What the hell? As long as he couldn't outrun the horse, he might as well face its rider and get this over with, right here and right now.

The rider had halted the equine and it stood obediently still, its head held high as if waiting for its next command. Jackson looked over the fine beast and then his eyes scanned the rider from boot to hat, his clothes, neat and clean, and a friendly grin adorning his rosy cheeks. He looked to be not much older than Jackson.

Hans Logan had always been a tall, gangly youngster, and now at age twenty, he had matured to a splendid looking young man with remarkable blond hair and more remarkable blue eyes. Muscular and agile, his features were clean-cut, his stature always erect and dignified.

His positive attitude and good common sense—not to mention that he was quite intelligent—had convinced Sheriff McMillan a year and a half ago to hire him as a deputy. And now there was a new sheriff, but Sheriff Colby liked the young deputy, too, and decided he could stay.

And he had a fine horse. The colt had been a birthday present from his father. He raised it, broke it, and trained it without any help. Hans was proud of the stallion he called Argo, after the ship in Greek Mythology sailed by Jason to recover the Golden Fleece.

"You new here?" the rider asked.

Reluctant at first, Jackson hesitated, but then he realized this was just a cordial greeting, and not one of hostility. He nodded and spoke meekly. "Well, yeah, I guess I am."

"Thought so... hadn't seen you 'round before."

"Just came in on the train this morning."

"Where from?"

"La Crosse."

"Just visiting?"

"No... I start working for Mr. Abernathy next Monday."

The rider dismounted, stepped around the front of his horse and patted its face, and then approached Jackson. It was then that Jackson noticed the gold medallion pinned to the breast of the rider's leather jacket. It had been hidden from his view until now. But before he allowed himself to process the whole thought, he blurted out, "D'ya always carry a gun?"

"Naw... just when I'm out huntin' criminals."

"Criminals?"

Hans had already gained a reputation with his clever method of tracking down a horse thief, but he would never boast about it because he knew it had been more luck than skill.

But his reputation didn't end there; he was known far and near for his marksmanship. Use of rifle and revolver seemed to be born in him; he was a natural master of firearms.

Offering his right hand, the rider said, "I'm Deputy Hans Logan. What's your name?"

Deputy? Jackson thought. *But he looks like only a kid... like me.* He accepted the handshake.

"Cat got your tongue? You weren't expecting me to be a lawman?"

"N—n—no. I guess I wasn't. Have I done something

wrong?"

"Of course not. Just wanted to say hello."

"Oh... well... in that case... I'm Jackson Evans." He breathed a little easier now that he better understood the circumstances. "You say you're out hunting criminals? What kind of criminals?"

"Oh, just some livestock rustlers. There's been a few head of cattle and sheep turned up missing over in Vernon County. And every time—about the time of the thievery—a stranger with a team and wagon has been seen heading back this way, so they think he's from 'round here somewhere. But no one's ever gotten a good look at him—always been at night."

Jackson, still overwhelmed with the deputy's youthful appearance couldn't hold back his next remark. "You look kinda young to be a deputy."

Deputy Logan chuckled. "I'm twenty. And I'd guess you to be a couple years younger."

"Seventeen."

"Okay... we're even." After a brief pause, Deputy Logan asked, "You stayin' out at Abernathy's place?"

"No... he said he don't have a bunkhouse. So I'm staying at Mrs. Jorgenson's boarding house... over on Franklin Street."

"Oh, sure," Logan replied. "I know the place."

Jackson retrieved his watch from a pocket. He'd burned up another half hour. By the time he walked back to the boarding house, washed up a bit and combed his hair, it would be time for supper... that his stomach still reminded him he desperately needed. He offered his hand again. "It's a pleasure meeting you, Deputy Hans Logan," he said as he glanced at his watch again. "I don't mean to be rude, but I gotta get back now for supper. Haven't eaten all day since breakfast."

"Don't blame you none," the deputy replied. He stepped closer to his horse as if to release himself from the conversation. When he was in the saddle again, he turned and called out to Jackson, who was only a few steps away. "Hey, Jackson. My friends call me Logan. I'll see ya 'round, okay?"

Jackson waved. "Okay... Logan."

When he had strolled half the distance back to the house, pleased with the outcome, he realized how professionally Logan had handled their meeting. Logan had noticed a stranger in town—who could have been a dangerous criminal—and in such a clever way of conducting the conversation, he had learned everything he needed to know: Jackson's name; how old he was; where he came from, and what he was doing in town; where he would be working and staying. Not that Jackson objected. He hoped he had made another good friend, and that he *would* see him again.

Chapter 5

A bell hung from the ceiling on the front porch, and at six o'clock sharp, Jackson learned of its function. Loud clangs erupted from the bell as thunderous footsteps fell on the staircase, their creators in high anticipation of partaking of the meal, from which aromas were now permeating the entire house. With scrubbed face and hands, and perfectly combed hair, Jackson followed the others to the dining room where two maids cordially showed everyone to their seats. The long table was set with plates, tumblers, napkins and silverware on a white linen tablecloth. At the center were small bowls of butter and jam and pickles, and plates of sliced bread.

The huge oak table could accommodate at least a dozen people, but this night, only eight—including Jackson—sat down to eat. He quickly scanned the faces around the table, only three of which he recognized. At the far end of the table sat Jacob, who he had only seen on the porch that afternoon, sound asleep and snoring. Sitting directly across from him was a porter he had seen earlier at the railroad depot, but he didn't know his name. Next to him was the man from the Haberdashery, Victor Johnson. Jackson smiled and acknowledged Mr. Johnson when their eyes met, and Victor returned the kindly gesture.

Then the depot porter reached across the table offering his hand. "Hi. I'm Henry Good," he said as they shook hands.

"Yes," the boy answered. "I'm Jackson Evans. I think I saw you at the railroad depot this morning. I just came from La Crosse today."

This appeared to be strictly a men's dwelling house, as the only women Jackson had seen, so far, was Millie Jorgenson and the two maids. Just then Millie and her helpers came through the doorway carrying platters of fare that had provided delicious cooking smells all afternoon, the best of all being the one containing the golden roasted goose. The meal was served family style, with the plates and platters passed from one diner to another until everyone had plenty of food on their plates. While the serving was going on, Millie announced their new guest, Jackson Evans. She stood behind him and caressed his shoulders as a mother would caress a child. "I know you all vill like Jackson," she said. "I hope you all vill have a chance to introduce yourselves and make him feel velcome."

Everyone nodded and smiled in Jackson's direction, but it was perfectly clear they were here to eat first and ask questions later. And with the first few bites of his meal, Jackson understood why. The food was superb, easily rivaling his mother's cooking. As the new guest he was offered a leg from the roast goose. The meat almost melted in his mouth, and the corn and beans tasted like they had been just picked from the garden. The apple sauce had the perfect amount of cinnamon and just the right sweetness; the bread, light and oven-fresh. Jackson knew, now, without any doubt, that he *had* struck a bonanza.

When the men had had their fill, and the final offering of extra helpings was waved away, some of them went out on the porch to smoke their pipes, and others retired to the sitting room for the usual evening social gathering. Jackson was naturally the center ring attraction as questions spewed out. They wanted to know everything about him, and he obliged with stories about his life in La Crosse and about his father's absence all winter while he worked in the logging camps up north. He told about climbing the bluffs, and about watching the progress every day when the railroad trestle was built across the Black and Mississippi Rivers. He was only eight years old then, but he remembered it quite well.

He held everyone's attention for a couple of hours, and then one by one the gentlemen left the parlor for their rooms upstairs. When only a couple remained, one of them, Reverend Thomas Thorp asked, "So Jackson... have you met any of the other town folk yet?"

"Well, yeah," Jackson replied. "I met Victor Johnson at the Haberdashery, and I met Ted at the General Store—he's the one who told me about this place—and of course I met Mr. Abernathy, my employer." He thought a moment, and then continued. "Oh, yeah, and I met Deputy Hans Logan."

"Aaah, Hans Logan. Now there's a fine young man. You can't go wrong if you keep Logan as your friend."

Chapter 6

Charlie McCoy lay quietly in his hotel room guarding a reputation, unsure if it had preceded him. He reflected on the years he spent in and out of Deadwood Gulch in the Dakota Territory where his life had taken many turns, gaining fortunes in various endeavors, and losing them just as quickly in the many Deadwood gambling halls.

Many men of the new American frontier country were eager to escape the restrictions of their former environment and wanted an identity of their own. In the process of achieving it, they produced a unique character. They lived off the land, abided by their own rules, and owed allegiance to no one. Having severed their ties with the old civilization, they were also free of its responsibilities.

From this group, constantly pushing farther west was a smaller group of men trying to escape the net of civilization and the arm of the law. They were forever crossing the line, always living on the edge. This was Charlie McCoy.

He came from among the thousands of unemployed easterners who drifted to the west, only to find jobs scarce there, too. Some found work in the cattle industry and farm labor, and some turned to crime. But whatever the profession, they all led a sort of nomadic life. They became self-reliant and hardened by the continuous fight for survival.

When he fist arrived in Deadwood, he soon learned that the town was indeed lawless. Even rougher than Dodge City, Kansas, it was a town born of gold fever in a territory that was not yet part of the United States. Its Main Street was established with businesses owned by men who would rather not have the law present—brothels, saloons and gambling houses that were quite proficient at separating the miners from their gold dust and nuggets with methods not always honest or honorable.

Charlie had been in town only a few days when he wondered into Saloon Number 10 for a cool beer. Moments later he heard behind him the deafening blast from Jack McCall's .44 that abruptly ended Wild Bill Hickok's life. It was at that very moment that he began to understand the reality of the harshness characteristic of the Black Hills at the time. With no lawmen—and no law—killings were frequent; some went unquestioned, not even investigated, and many went unpunished. Those that didn't escape punishment were usually at the hands of friends seeking revenge or self-proclaimed justice.

Deadwood Gulch was, in essence, a safe haven for crooks, as long as they stayed on the good side of men like Al Swearengen, the owner of the Gem Theater. Until Seth Bullock became Deadwood's first sheriff, Al Swearengen was the law, being the wealthiest, most influential, and hence, the most powerful man in the town.

Charlie heard rumors that Jack McCall had been "influenced" and that Wild Bill Hickok's death, and the death of Preacher Henry Smith a few days later had occurred because they were among the very few decent people in Deadwood who preferred and promoted law and order. Jack McCall, though, proclaimed he had killed Hickok to avenge his brother's death by Wild Bill's gun when Hickok was a Texas lawman, and the Preacher's demise was blamed on

Indians, although there was never any proof established to support either claim.

By then, all the good mining claims were taken. Charlie saw little hope of making his fortune panning for gold. But he had struck upon another idea. Winter would soon be blowing its cold, bitter wrath, smothering Deadwood under a blanket of ice and snow and frigid temperatures. Even these hot-blooded hotheads would need fuel for their stoves and fireplaces.

With nearly all the money he had left, Charlie traded his riding horse for a sturdy team, bought a wagon, axes and saws, and started harvesting a different kind of gold—firewood—that lay in abundance throughout the surrounding hills. And when the icy winds began to chill the gambling rooms, Charlie could nearly name his price for a cord of firewood.

His efforts through the winter months earned him comfortable living quarters, three square meals a day, and a handsome profit. But this bonanza could only last until spring.

Charlie had made acquaintance with another trio who came from Texas. Sam Bass, Joel Collins, and Jack Davis didn't seem the typical cattle drivers, but they claimed to have made quite a large profit on a herd of 500 head they bought in Texas, and sold at the railhead in Kansas. In short order they had lost most of the money at the gambling tables. Collins had built a good house in Deadwood and sent for his mistress, Maude, whom he moved north from a brothel in Dallas. He and Bass started a freighting business between Cheyenne and Deadwood, but it proved less than a profitable venture. In the meantime, the house had become a notorious brothel and popular hangout for a band of Sam's desperado friends—Jim Berry, Bill Heffridge, Tom Nixon, Frank Towle, and Robert McKimie. They all eventually became known as the "Collins Gang." With a failing freight business and the results of Maude's efforts not enough to support their wild lifestyles, the gang looked to other means of gaining working capital.

On their first attempt in late March to hold up the Black Hills Stage and Express Line carrying gold out of Deadwood, a critical mistake made by one of the gang members, Robert McKimie, prevented the robbery to even occur. As the stagecoach came slowly around a bend in the trail, McKimie fired his shotgun, instantly killing the driver and injuring a passenger sitting beside him. At the sound of gunfire, the frightened horses bolted, taking the stage, its passengers, and precious cargo quickly out of range and away from danger. Another notorious road agent was immediately suspected of the attempted robbery and murder, giving the Black Hills Bandits time to regroup.

McKimie was kicked out of the gang and ordered to leave Deadwood, which he did without hesitation. He knew if he didn't leave, he would probably find an early grave.

After six more stagecoach heists netting little more that pocket change and a few watches, Collins and his Black Hills Bandits decided they needed something bigger, and they started making plans to rob a train. But there weren't any trains in the Dakota Territory, so they stole a string of strong horses and six of them rode off for Nebraska unnoticed.

They arrived near Ogallala in early September and camped a short distance from the depot for a week while laying out a train robbery scheme. Collins, who had taken on the role as leader, based the plan on his experience with robbing stagecoaches, finding a place where the train was stopped or could be stopped and easily boarded. After watching the movements of the trains for a week, the Big Springs Station several miles west of town seemed to be the most logical choice for the attack.

Early one September morning the six men rode to within a half-mile of the station, hid their horses in the woods, and waited all day. The eastbound Union Pacific train No. 4 from San Francisco to Chicago was due to arrive at 10:48 PM. A little after 10, under the cover of darkness, they rode to the station, and at gunpoint held the station agent captive and forced him to destroy his telegraph key. When they heard the whistle in the distance, they made the agent place a red lantern on the tracks, a signal of danger that no engineer would ignore. The train stopped at the platform. Collins and Heffridge then captured the engineer and fireman and took them inside the station to be guarded with the station agent by a couple of the other gang members. Then they joined Sam Bass and Jack Davis in the express car. It was then that they realized their efforts were hampered by a time lock on the safe. The express agent couldn't open it... even with the threat of a six-gun pointed at his head.

After Sam's futile attempt to break the lock with an axe, he searched the rest of the express car's contents and found three wooden boxes sealed with wax and addressed from the mint at San Francisco to a New York bank. He quickly busted them open to find $20,000 in newly minted gold coins in each box.

But they could hear another train approaching, and to avoid further risk of capture, they released all the railroad men and sent the train on its way. The gang then made their successful getaway to a remote spot in the Nebraska dunes where they divided the loot. To make tracking more difficult for lawmen, they split up in pairs and all rode off in different directions. They could meet again later when things cooled down.

Tom Nixon and Jim Berry started out together. Nixon, after several hours' ride, told Berry he was heading for Florida and left his companion. But when they were separated a safe distance, Nixon turned north toward the Great Lakes and Canada. He was counting on never seeing any of the others again, and he certainly didn't intend ever return to Deadwood. He covered his trail so well that for several years, even the Pinkertons were quite dismayed that he had escaped successfully out of the country with ten thousand dollars of Union Pacific's money.

Chapter 7

Eager to start his new job, Jackson hiked the road east out of town in the crisp, refreshing air. Expecting to find himself among a large crew of woodcutters when he arrived at Mr. Abernathy's place, he was a bit puzzled when he saw only one other man with the farmer. It was the same man Mr. Abernathy had hired just before him, Charlie McCoy.

Jackson quickly surveyed the farmstead; several stacks of hay, a large granary, a low barn with a few horses, a couple milk cows and a half-dozen beef cattle corralled around it, and a small frame house that had not yet seen a coat of paint. Behind the house stood a stone smokehouse, and at the foot of the hill just beyond, a spring house, out of which ran a small trickle of a stream that meandered from the hillside and fed a pond inside the corral. A pair of wild mallards that seemed unconcerned with the domestic animals paddled in the pond, and a few chickens wandered aimlessly about, as if in search for anything edible. But nowhere did he see any other tree cutting crew.

Mr. Abernathy greeted him as he approached. "Mornin' Mr. Evans," he said cheerfully, extending his hand. "Charlie McCoy... Jackson Evans," the farmer introduced his new employees. They shook hands. "You two will be working together, and I guess you know what you'll be doing so we won't waste any time explaining that. Let's get your tools loaded in a wagon, and I'll drive you out to the timber so you can get started."

They marched over to the barn where Mr. Abernathy opened a door and quickly started handing axes, wedges, saws, block-and-tackle, peaveys, pry bars, and various ropes out to Jackson and Charlie. They in turn loaded the implements into a wagon standing next to the doorway. When the task was complete, the farmer disappeared for a few minutes, and then came out another doorway leading a harnessed team of draft horses. The trained team responded perfectly to his gentle commands as he backed them to the wagon. When they were in position, he hitched the wagon tongue, tied the reigns to the front of the wagon and started climbing aboard. "Jump on boys," he called out.

After about a half-mile ride across the valley they came to a small shed that Mr. Abernathy had built earlier. They were near the La Crosse River where the soil was rich and level—perfect for cropland except for all the oak and hickory trees. It wasn't a thick forest, but enough trees to make farming the land impossible.

"This is where you'll start, boys," Mr. Abernathy said. "You can work your way back from the river toward my buildings."

Jackson gazed back to where the farm buildings stood against the hillside. Hundreds of trees dotted the land, and Jackson imagined that he would be there cutting timber for the rest of his life.

They unloaded the tools and equipment into the shelter. "You can keep everything here," Mr. Abernathy said. "No need to haul them out here every day." Then he went on to explain that he wanted all the good logs saved for lumber, and the large limbs could be cut into firewood, and all the junk that was left could be piled up and burned. "Any questions?" he asked.

Charlie and Jackson shook their heads. "Only one thing," Charlie said. "We quit at five o'clock... earlier if it's really cold."

"I have no problem with that," the boss said, and then he drove the team and wagon away toward his buildings.

Charlie McCoy was a little different from any of the people Jackson had known while growing up. He possessed a sort of racy, reckless, individual liberty that supported a freedom from restraints of society. He was poised and self-sufficient, and his attitude toward just about everything was not exactly suspicious, but rather, watchful. Only when he was assured that other people understood his position was he willing to enter into any relationship. But Jackson had not yet learned all this about Charlie. He wasn't giving too much of himself away, even to Jackson, to whom it seemed he had taken a liking, although Jackson didn't know why.

He wore a heavy charcoal gray felt hat; the crown deeply creased down the middle and a broad brim—said it turns away the sun better than straw. A big, bulky, brightly-colored silk handkerchief around his neck he said kept the sun off and the dust out. Leather gauntlets protected his hands.

"Why a *silk* handkerchief?" Jackson asked.

"Ever seen a drought? If you have, then you know it's some kinda dusty. And some places out in the western deserts there's been a drought for a hundred and seven million years come next July."

Jackson chuckled.

"Now you go drive a couple thousand head of cattle—and they've got four feet each—why, the dust gets so thick your horse can't fall down when he stumbles. That 'kerchief tied around your neck, coverin' your nose and mouth filters out the dust. It's not just an ornament. And *silk*, not just 'cause it's pretty, but 'cause it's better to breath through."

As the days wore on and the pair learned each other's working abilities, their efforts became more and more harmonious. They could anticipate next moves, and soon their motions were like a well-engineered machine. It allowed them to talk about other things, and still accomplish the work they were expected to do. Most of the time it was Charlie doing most of the talking, telling stories in answer to Jackson's questions.

"So, what'd ya do before you came here?"

"Oh, I was a cow puncher out in Montana for a spell."

"Why'd ya leave there?"

"Well, the cattle rancher I worked for lost most of his herd in a bad winter. Didn't need all his hired hands after that."

"What happened to the cattle?"

"Froze to death. It was forty below zero. Them that survived the cold starved 'cause there was so much snow they couldn't get to food."

"So what'd you do? Stand around and watch cows eat grass all day?"

Charlie heaved out a hearty belly laugh. "No, there's more to it than that. I was a line rider most of the time."

"What's a line rider do?"

"We stayed in little shacks along the perimeter of the grazing land. The shacks were about two miles apart. I'd ride as far as the next shack and then back again to watch for strays wandering off."

"Must've been lonely."

"Naw... saw the rider at the next shack sometimes couple times a day. And the supply wagon showed up every couple of weeks."

"Sounds boring."

"Peaceful is what it was...'cept for when a couple Injuns tried rustlin' off a few head of strays."

"What happened? What'd ya do?"

"Me and Lenny—the rider at the next shack—caught up with 'em. Had a little shoot-out, but we finally scared 'em off."

"Get the cows back?"

"They scattered when the shootin' started. We rounded up all of 'em 'cept one, and I think a mountain lion got that one. We found bones and big cat tracks the next day."

Jackson was intrigued with Charlie's stories; they told of another culture that fascinated him. For the first time, all the tales he'd read in the newspapers about the wild west came to life when told by someone who had actually been there, who had experienced the frontier wilderness, and survived. He began to recognize Charlie as a role model—the kind of toughness he needed to learn. He decided he wanted to be more like Charlie, and at his first opportunity, he went to see Victor at the Haberdashery.

"Still got those silk handkerchiefs?" he asked.

"Sure. Changed your mind, did you?"

"Well, Charlie says the silk is better to breathe through

when you tie it over your face to keep the sawdust out."

Then on a bone-chilling Friday afternoon when they were about to quit for the day, Charlie invited Jackson to join him at the North Star Saloon for a drink.

"But I don't have much money left till payday," Jackson said. "And my room rent is due tomorrow."

"Not a problem," said McCoy. "I have plenty of money. I'll by you a beer."

The saloon was a favorite meeting place for farmers and town folk alike. There they could combine business and pleasure. Entertainment was limited, but the proprietor endeavored to appeal to all types of clientele, serving imported liquor, wines, and various beers, including Guinness from Ireland.

It was housed in a modest frame structure about forty feet long and thirty feet wide. The bar with its polished brass rail ran along the left side from the front entrance, and behind it against the wall was a mantle with bottles and decanters of various liquors and wines, all polished and shimmering like diamonds. Opposite the bar along the other wall were scattered small round tables and chairs, and near the back was a billiard table. The floor was sprinkled with sawdust, and over the room hung the characteristic saloon odor—a combination of stale beer, sweat, and tobacco smoke.

The warmth from the potbelly stove felt good after spending the day out in the cold. Jackson lingered there warming his hands while Charlie ordered two glasses of beer from the saloonkeeper.

"This place kinda reminds me of Saloon Number Ten, out in Deadwood."

"You were in Deadwood?"

"Oh, sure. Spent three or four years there."

"Did ya pan for gold?"

"No. All the good claims were taken by the time I got there."

"So... what'd you do?"

"Cut and sold firewood. Gets mighty cold out there."

"Did you know Wild Bill Hickok?"

"Yep. He was one of the first people I met there. And I was at the saloon the day Jack McCall murdered him." Charlie went on to tell the gruesome details of the event, and Jackson soaked it all in.

When his beer glass was empty and Charlie's story was finished, he excused himself. "Don't want to be late for supper. I think Millie's cookin' a pot roast tonight."

Chapter 8

J ackson welcomed a couple of days off after a week of sawing and chopping. He enjoyed being out in the fresh air, but it *was* hard work, and a few muscles needed some rest. After a hearty breakfast of beef hash and eggs, he sat on the front porch alone and watched the sunrise over the distant hills. Victor Johnson, the haberdasher, and Henry Good, the railroad depot porter stepped out the front door.

"Well, good morning, Jackson," Victor said as they passed. "Looks like a glorious day. Not working today?"

"Nope... day off."

The two men strolled past the only green thing left in sight, the cedar hedge, and then on up the street toward town. Jackson watched them until they reached Leonard Street where they separated—Victor heading to his store and Henry turning toward the depot.

Saturday morning sunshine came in intervals as lazy white clouds drifted from west to east pushed by a chilly November wind, and a November wind could not be trusted. It might usher in anything from icy rain to fluffy snow. Winter was near, although the clouds this day didn't appear particularly threatening.

Contemplating the odds of a blizzard swooping into the valley, his thoughts drifted to his home in La Crosse, his mother and his two brothers, Jeffery and John. He worried about them being there alone with winter coming on; before he left, he and his father had made sure the woodshed was full so they had plenty of firewood to keep them warm all winter. The cellar was stocked with all the vegetables from their garden, just like every year. Jeff and John were old enough now to help out with chores, and if any big problem arose, there were lots of good neighbors close by. But still, he was concerned.

He wondered what he would find to do all day—with *two* days. A bit of loneliness stumbled around inside him.

Then a voice calling his name interrupted his thoughts. "Hey, Jackson." He was so deep in his daydream that the voice didn't register right away. "Hey, Jackson! Aren't you going to work today?"

He sprang himself back to reality and looked up to see Deputy Logan and his magnificent horse just beyond the cedar hedge. "No," he answered as he trotted down the steps to meet his new friend. "No, I don't work on Saturdays or Sundays."

"Well then," Logan said. "Wanna go for a ride?" Then as an afterthought he added, "You *can* ride a horse, can't you?"

"Sure. I ride the neighbor's horses a lot back home."

"Well? Do you want to go for a ride with me?" Logan repeated.

"Sure," Jackson said. "But I don't have a horse here."

"That's okay," Logan said. "I have another one you can ride. I'll be back in half an hour." And with that said he was turned and riding away.

"Where are we going?" Jackson asked with his voice raised a little in excitement.

"I'll tell you when I get back," Logan replied over his shoulder.

Jackson just stood there a few moments, watching Logan ride away, puzzled at first. But then a warm feeling washed over him and his mouth curled into a big smile. He forgot about the chilly air. He forgot about the needless worry for his family in La Crosse. And most of all, he forgot about being lonely. That man he had met on the train— Theodore—had been absolutely right. He'd found a friend, or more accurately, a friend had found him, and a good one, one worth keeping according to Reverend Thomas Thorp, anyway. And who would be more knowing about such matters than him?

With the jubilance of a school boy at recess, he spun around quickly, intending to fetch his warm jacket with the fur collar from is room. He collided with the Reverend whom he was unaware had come out of the house and approached him from behind on the walkway. The impact caused the preacher to drop a well-worn leather-bound Bible and an equally worn leather covered notebook. They went crashing to the ground.

"Oh! Reverend! I'm so sorry!" exclaimed Jackson. He gained his composure and rapidly collected the books at his feet, brushed away the dust and dry leaf fragments from their covers, and with flowing apology said, "I didn't know you were there. What are you doing out so early?"

"I was spying on you."

"You were?"

"Of course not! I was just on my way to the church to prepare for tomorrow's service. I saw you were having a conversation with Hans Logan just before I came out."

"Yes. He's coming back in a little while with another horse. We're going for a ride."

"Where?"

"Don't rightly know. Said he'd tell me later."

The preacher snugged his coat collar tighter around his

neck and adjusted his black hat to better protect him from the chilly breeze. "Kinda nippy out here this morning," he said evaluating Jackson's attire that, to him, seemed a little inadequate for the weather. "Better put on some warmer clothes, then."

Jackson handed the books to Reverend Thorp when his hands were once again free. "Yes... Thank you... I will... in fact I was on my way to get my coat when I bumped into you. And I *really* am sorry about that."

"Oh, don't be. I shouldn't have snuck up on you like that. Well, you and Hans enjoy your ride."

"Thank you, Reverend. We will."

The preacher passed through the opening in the hedge and Jackson started back to the house to retrieve his coat. The preacher stopped, turned, and called to the boy. "If you have nothing too pressing tomorrow morning, you're welcome to attend our church service."

Jackson looked back from the porch steps. "Thank you, Reverend. I might do that."

He was waiting on the porch with the rabbit fur collar of his warm jacket turned up around his neck when Logan appeared again, this time leading another fine-looking gelding, saddled and ready for the journey, the destination of which Jackson was still clueless.

Logan tossed the reins down to Jackson. "His name's Apollo. He's pretty gentle. You shouldn't have any trouble with him."

Jackson took the reins. "Hello, Apollo," he said to the creature and gently caressed the side of its head. Apollo seemed to acknowledge the greeting with a responsive, quiet nicker.

"Yeah," Logan said. "I think he likes you okay."

Jackson put a foot in the stirrup, swung into the saddle, looked at Logan and said, "Well? What are we waiting for? Let's go."

Logan led them east out of town past the stockyards that were quite busy this time of year.

"Funny," Jackson said as they rode past the pens full of cattle.

"What's funny?" asked Logan.

"That Charlie didn't get a job here working with the cattle instead of cuttin' trees."

"Who's Charlie?"

"Charlie McCoy... the guy I work with out at Abernathy's place."

"Oh, *that* Charlie. Why is it funny?"

"Well, 'cause he said he used to work on a cattle ranch out in Montana."

Logan's eyes narrowed as if in deep thought. By then they were well past the noise of the stockyards. "That *is* funny," he said.

"Why do you say that?"

"He told me he came from Michigan."

"You've talked to him?"

"Sure."

"Well, yeah, he probably did come from Michigan. The work in Montana was a long time ago."

Logan just nodded.

"Say... where are we going, anyway?" Jackson asked.

"A little town called Norwalk, about twenty miles other side of Sparta."

"I've heard of it... and why are we going there?"

"Sheriff Colby wants me to ride over there and take a look around."

"Oh! So you're working today."

"Sort of."

About a half-hour later they trotted through the Village of Bangor, and in another half-hour they rode into Rockland just as a westbound mail train pulled into the depot. Right in the middle of town was a water trough where they dismounted and let the horses drink as much as they wanted.

Jackson had admired Logan's horse all morning, how smooth and graceful, and how its coat shimmered in the sunlight, and how it and Logan seemed to move as one.

"You never told me his name," Jackson said.

"Huh?"

"His name... you never told me your horse's name."

"Oh! This is Argo."

The steed turned his head at the sound of his name.

"Argo. Apollo. Where did you get these names?"

"They're form Greek mythology. Did you ever read any Greek mythology in school?" He took a drink from a canteen and handed it to Jackson.

"No, not that I remember."

"Apollo is the god of the sun. And I named Argo after the ship that Jason sailed in pursuit of the Golden Fleece."

When Argo and Apollo seemed to have quenched their thirst, Logan suggested they should be on their way again. The boys swung into their saddles and galloped up the trail to Sparta. There they turned into the hazy hills that seemed to roll on forever to the south.

The *Chicago and North Western* tracks came into view now and then as they followed the wagon road that, as Logan explained, was the route the stagecoaches traveled before the railroads came. But now, many trains every day steamed and whistled through the valleys and over the hills—with a little help from the pusher engines kept at Kendall, another small town to the east where the steep hills began. There was no need for stagecoaches on this road anymore.

They found a spot along the trail to stop for a short rest. The sun was higher now, and they were in a valley protected from the wind. The temperature had risen considerably, and the day was turning out to be quite pleasant for November.

They tied Argo and Apollo to saplings and then sat upon a large boulder alongside the trail. Jackson had noticed earlier that Logan was armed. He couldn't help but comment about the holstered revolver at his side. "So, I guess you must be out hunting a dangerous outlaw today, eh?"

"Don't know if he's dangerous... why do you ask?"

"'Cause of the sidearm hangin' on your belt. Remember? You told me you carried a gun whenever you were huntin' dangerous outlaws."

"Oh, that. Well, the sheriff said I should always have my revolver. Never know what you might run into these days."

"Guess there's lots of stuff you gotta know to be a deputy, eh, Logan?"

Logan shrugged his shoulders. "Yeah, I s'pose there is," he said in a modest tone.

Jackson was beginning to understand his growing admiration of Logan: not just because he was a deputy sheriff who carried a gun, or because he had a pair of fine riding horses. It was more because of how Logan had almost immediately accepted their friendship, and he seemed truly interested in making it stronger. There was no other apparent reason for inviting someone he barely knew to accompany him on this outing.

"So, what would you do if a dangerous outlaw walked up to you right now?"

Logan grinned. "Guess I'd offer him a handshake and invite him to sit down on this rock beside me."

Jackson threw him a questioning stare.

"You see, Jackson, he probably ain't a dangerous outlaw."

Jackson squinted and his stare became more intense. "How do you know that?"

"Well, you should never overlook the most obvious. A dangerous criminal doesn't usually walk up to a man with a badge on his chest and introduce himself."

Jackson squinted some more and groaned, knowing that Logan had outsmarted him. But he had not tried to belittle Jackson by saying that the question wasn't thought out or very intelligent. Instead, he had given an answer that didn't offend.

Argo and Apollo started getting restless. Logan knew they weren't particularly satisfied in their confinement; they wanted to run. He rose from his perch on the rock, stepped toward Argo and patted the horse's neck. "Okay, Boy," he said soothingly. "We'll go now," he said to Jackson. "It's about another hour's ride from here."

When they arrived at Norwalk, Logan knew right where to go to hear the local gossip. He'd been at the Norwalk General Store many times. By now all the local gentlemen who generally gathered around the potbelly stove on a bitter winter day or in the shade under the front awning in the sweltering summer recognized him as a competent deputy. They showed their respect for his position even if they thought he was a little young for such a job.

It didn't take Jackson long to determine that Logan's reputation shone bright and clear. The Reverend Thomas Thorp certainly knew how to judge a person's character, and so for, Jackson could find no reason to disagree. The men seated on stools and wooden boxes formed a circle around what appeared to be an empty packing crate turned on its side, upon which sat several tin coffee cups within easy reach of the men sitting there. When Logan and Jackson entered the store the tiny bell attached to the top of the door announced their arrival, and the men all turned toward them and greeted Logan as if he were one of them. "Hello, Logan," one older man said. "You come to catch some dirty scoundrel trouble maker?"

"Hello, Amos," Logan returned with a smile. Then he made his way around the circle, patting shoulders, shaking hands and greeting each one there by his first name. "Don't know that I'll catch one today, but if you know of one hangin' around, I'll sure commence looking for him," he finally said and then headed to the man behind the counter.

"Good to see you, Deputy Logan." The store owner gave Logan a friendly smile and offered his hand.

"Hello, Jonas. How are things in Norwalk these days? Any trouble?"

"Nope. Quiet 'n peaceful."

"Heard of any cattle missing?"

"Not 'round here, but I heard there's trouble like that down in Vernon County."

"Yeah," Logan said. "I've heard that, too." Then he eyed a big jar filled with beef jerky on a shelf behind the counter. "I'll take some of that jerky," he said, digging in his pocket for money.

Jonas placed the jar on the counter and unscrewed the lid. Logan reached in and grabbed a handful. "How much, Jonas?"

"Oh, two bits is fine."

Logan handed the storekeeper the money. "Okay, Jonas. I'll be heading out now. If you hear of any trouble, you let us know."

"Thanks, Logan. I'll do that... and it's real good to see you again."

Logan gave half of the jerky to Jackson. As they passed by the group around the stove he bid his farewell to them. They all grinned and waved. "So long, Logan. Don't be a stranger."

They rode up and down all the streets of Norwalk. Jackson knew that Logan was probably keeping an eye out for a particular wagon, but he didn't seem to observe anything that drew his attention.

It was mid-afternoon when they rode into Sparta. Bright sunshine from a clear sky had warmed the day to a pleasant Indian summer, and the town hummed with activity of the many people taking advantage of the nice weather.

"There's Sheriff Colby' horse," Logan said as they passed the grist mill along the La Crosse River. He pointed to the distinctly yellow-colored palomino mare with blonde mane and tail tied to a hitching post in front of the mill. "I need to talk to him, but I won't be long. Wait for me."

Jackson dismounted from Apollo. He watched Logan tie Argo to a hitching post and sprint to the open mill door where he disappeared into the depths of the structure. Just a few minutes passed and he came bounding out again, untied Argo and swung into the saddle.

"Let's go into town and eat," Logan said. "I'm starved."

Jackson didn't object. The long ride had made him hungry.

Chapter 9

The weeks passed and the snow came, and to Jackson, Mr. Abernathy's buildings didn't seem to be getting any closer. But there also seemed to be an ample supply of stories from Charlie, and that always made the days pass quickly, especially when the temperature dropped and they went back to town early. There was always a warm fire at the North Star Saloon, and a warm brandy and a beer was a good way to end the day.

"Y' know, Charlie," Jackson said one evening at the bar. "There's always a good hot meal at the boarding house where I live. Two dollars a week, and you could have yourself some good home cooking every night."

"I don't want to live in no boarding house," Charlie said. "I'm perfectly happy at the hotel."

"You don't have to live there to eat there. Millie has lots of people at her table who don't live there."

"Food's good, eh?" Charlie was having second thoughts.

"Yeah. I hear it's the best in town."

"Well, I guess I could give it a try."

"Good! I'll tell Millie tonight so she'll have enough for one more tomorrow night."

And so, from then on, all winter Charlie came to the boarding house for breakfast and supper. Millie was grateful for the extra income, although she didn't really care for Charlie's stories about Deadwood killings and Dodge City shoot-outs at the supper table. But she tolerated it because it seemed to entertain some of the other boarders.

Just like he had promised, Jackson went home for the Christmas holiday, and just like he had promised, with gifts for his mom and his two little brothers: a beautiful, warm wool scarf for Sarah, and mittens, candy and story books for Jeffery and John. When he returned, it was with a sense of accomplishment and satisfaction.

Nearly every Saturday morning, weather permitting, Logan arrived at the boarding house on Argo with Apollo trotting alongside saddled and ready. "The horses need some exercise," Logan would always say, but the real reason he came by was that he enjoyed Jackson's company. They'd ride off to different towns, and sometimes just explore the hills. If the weather was too cold or snowy, they would sometimes join the other men in the boarding house parlor for checkers or cards. Jackson was often invited to the Logan home for a family supper. Otis and Ingrid Logan took an immediate liking to Jackson and told him he was always welcome. Their home was large and somewhat luxurious, and it had a warm, comforting feel. Jackson liked to spend time there; the warm family spirit reminded him of his home in La Crosse.

Chapter 10

"D'ya think you have the guts to make money without working for it?" Charlie McCoy asked his young partner.

Jackson Evans took a bite of his jerky, chewed at it a bit, and then took an interest as Charlie's question sank in. "How?"

"Hear that whistle?" Charlie nodded his head toward the east. It was the familiar sound of the *Chicago, Milwaukee & St. Paul* steaming down the tracks less than a mile away.

Jackson listened to the whistle he had heard hundreds of times. "Yeah, I hear it."

"Rob a train," McCoy said.

Jackson stared at the grizzly sort of man he had known only a few months. In the span of about thirty seconds Jackson processed the thought and quickly abandoned it. He laughed at Charlie, thinking it was some sort of joke, picked up his end of the crosscut saw and started toward the next oak that was already notched and waiting to be felled.

McCoy saw that Jackson hadn't taken him seriously. But he knew that robbing a train held promise of riches and Jackson soon understood that Charlie wasn't about to let the idea die.

"We could pull it off, ya know..." he said while they sawed at the oak. "With a little help, we could be rich beyond your wildest dreams."

Jackson had never enjoyed the luxuries wealth could provide. Now he was beginning to realize that Charlie McCoy was serious about robbing a train. He said nothing. He just listened.

"I heard about lots o' train holdups out west... lots of men that got filthy rich."

Jackson briefly looked over at McCoy to see if the sincerity was still in his eyes. It seemed to be.

"There's always a lot of money in the safe in the express car, and all it takes to get it is a few men with guns and horses, a stick of dynamite to blow up the safe, grab the loot and disappear into the dark."

The big oak tree started to crackle and groan, and with a few more strokes of the saw blade, the timber went crashing to the ground.

Jackson remained silent, but McCoy could tell he was considering the possibilities. "So... what d'ya think? Would ya like t' wear fine clothes and live in a fancy house? Or do ya wanna keep on makin' a few lousy bucks for a month's worth of hard labor?"

"Let me think about it a while," Jackson replied.

"Okay, then. We'll talk about it tonight over a beer at the saloon," McCoy said. "After supper."

The warmer days of March offered more pleasant working conditions out in the woods, but it had been a long day, and later that night, after they had eaten supper at the boarding house, Jackson would have sooner just gone to his room and slept. But his curiosity had grown since that afternoon. After all, he was just a seventeen-year-old kid, and this was as far away from La Crosse as he'd ever been. McCoy was twelve years older, had traveled the country far and wide, and he seemed to know a lot about what was going on in the rest of the world. And he was probably right about staying poor, earning a few lousy dollars for a month's hard labor. The more he thought about it, the thrill of such a venture got his blood pumping, and now he was eagerly looking forward to the chat with Charlie McCoy at the saloon.

Charlie had wisely said nothing about robbing trains during supper so none of the other boarders there at the table would have any suspicions. And he certainly didn't want the proprietor, Millicent Jorgensen to hear any of it. She was known to gossip a bit.

He finished his meal long before Jackson, slapped Jackson on the back, and said, "I'll see ya at the North Star Saloon. There's somebody I have to talk to."

Jackson eyed the others around the table, only to notice they were staring at him. They all seemed to have noticed Charlie's gesture and remark as he left. Jackson was quite certain, though, that they could not possibly know the reason for him meeting Charlie at the saloon, but just the same, he could feel his face turning red. He had always disguised his visits to the saloon to everyone at the boarding house, because he thought he had a family reputation to protect.

When Jackson's parents, David and Sarah Evans first came to Wisconsin, La Crosse was a young town at the edge of the Western frontier. Both their families had left Galena, Illinois in '49 and came up the river in search of something better than lead mining when so many were chasing false dreams of gold in the far West.

As on any frontier, religion provided the settlers a sort of umbrella to help protect them from the elements of a harsh environment. David and Sarah were married in a log church on the La Crosse prairie in 1862, and even though David served with the Union Army and was absent for the next three years, they never gave up their beliefs during that time when it would have been so easy to let go.

Although they were somewhat private about their faith, their children were raised with the basic tenets of the church, and it all seemed so natural in their everyday life; good manners, respect for their neighbors, polite language, a strong belief in the importance of family, and a most profound dislike of intoxication. Not that David Evans was a teetotaler, for he had a taste now and then, but always in moderation.

Chapter 11

At the North Star, a man Jackson recognized as another woodcutter was just leaving a table in the corner where McCoy sat, but he didn't know the man's name. Jackson stepped up to the bar that he had visited many times during the past months. He tossed a nickel on the bar. "Draw me a beer, Joshua," he said to the barkeeper. When the mug was set before him, he grabbed it like an old regular and sauntered over to McCoy's table.

"So... you must've decided my idea wasn't so bad after all, eh?" McCoy said in a low voice.

"Well, there's a few things I'm wondering about. How are we gonna get horses and guns? And who's gonna help us? And how are we gonna get dynamite without somebody asking questions? And how—"

"Just keep your shirt on, boy," McCoy cut him off. "This here's 1885 and there's gettin' to be a lot of people around these parts. We'll find the help we need. It'll just take some plannin'... that's all."

Jackson took a sip of his beer and decided he would hear what McCoy had to say.

"Now, I've already covered the dynamite part... that fellow who just left."

"He's a woodcutter, ain't he?" Jackson asked.

"Yeah. His name is John Schultz, and he also specializes in diggin' stumps out of farmers' fields. He's got dynamite... and he's in."

The youngster got the picture now. McCoy did know

how to plan this thing.

"Take a look over yonder at the barkeep, Joshua," McCoy said.

Jackson turned to peer toward the bar. Joshua had just poured a shot of whisky for an old man who appeared to be rather drunk.

"Well, would you look at that, Sam," the saloonkeeper said to the old man, pointing at the window. "Looks like it's startin' to rain!"

The old drunk turned to look out the window, and as he did, Joshua yanked the drink from the bar and quietly replaced it with an empty glass.

Sam turned back to reach for his drink. His vision was a little impaired, and he couldn't tell if it really was raining, but he did see that his glass was empty. "Hey, where's my whisky?"

"Well, Sam, I guess you drank your whisky."

Seeming somewhat perplexed, Sam plunked more coins down on the bar. "Well, then... bedder pour 'nother one."

Joshua took the money and pretended to pour a drink below the bar, and then set the same full glass in front of Sam.

McCoy winked at Jackson. "Ya see?" he whispered. "Now there's a top notch thief. He's got a gun rack full o' rifles in the back room, and his partner has a livery stable full o' horses and wagons. I'll talk to them later."

And talk to them he did. After most of the other patrons had left for the night, and Joshua had hoodwinked Sam by selling him the same shot of whisky two or three more times, McCoy ambled up to the bar. Jackson remained seated at the table as instructed. He watched the two conversing in low whispers that he couldn't hear, and at one point noticed them glance his way. McCoy had apparently explained Jackson's involvement, and Joshua Avery nodded his approval.

Jackson stared at the two, one on each side of the bar. Both with dark, slicked-back hair and bushy black mustaches against hard sun-baked faces, they could have passed for brothers, and he wasn't certain which, but one of them had to be Satan himself. He wondered how and why he had let himself get drawn into such a scheme, but then he was just as puzzled by the thought that he couldn't ignore the opportunity to become rich.

Several minutes had gone by when another man entered through the back door from the alley. Fiery-red hair stuck out from beneath his ten-gallon black hat, and an equally red beard hid a good share of his face. Hard boot heels clicked across the wooden floor, and as he passed by, Jackson caught the smell of horses. This was Joshua's partner, Louis Reed, the livery stable owner. He joined the saloonkeeper and McCoy at the bar and quickly was engaged in their secretive conversation.

What Jackson didn't hear was the immediate and almost overwhelming interest in a train holdup from the two new gang members. That's what it was becoming now – a gang – and Joshua had a couple of friends who were just the type to take an interest in such an opportunity. That would make their number seven.

Chapter 12

Several days passed while McCoy and Jackson returned to the tree cutting bright and early every morning. It seemed to Jackson that McCoy had all but lost his interest in trees and collecting a fair amount of pay at the end of the month. He knew what was on McCoy's mind, but Jackson held more confidence in what was real—the trees and the pay he would receive for cutting them down—than he did in the idea of robbing a train, even though it did intrigue him.

There was a foot of fresh white snow that had fallen overnight during a springtime storm. Snow disguised the contours of the land where mounds and false hills created a sense of solidness where there was none. From the middle of November to the end of February he had watched the snow pile up. He trudged through it, lugged tools around in it, and now he was sick of it.

Jackson was the fourth to arrive in the back room of the North Star Saloon about ten o'clock that night. Charlie McCoy, Joshua Avery, and Louis Reed sat on wooden chairs around the big table. There was a deck of cards and a pile of poker chips at the center of the table, but Jackson knew there would be little card playing that night. He slipped off his coat, draped it on the back of the chair next to McCoy, and feeling a bit intimidated by the older men he sat down.

"Hello, Jackson," Joshua said as he studied the boyish face that was not yet producing a beard. He had seen the young man in his barroom many times during the past couple of months, knew that he worked with Charlie McCoy, and now Charlie was counting him as a trustworthy partner in the train heist plan.

Jackson just nodded in acknowledgement of the greeting. He was just about to tell Charlie that he'd missed a delicious beef stew supper that Millie had served at the boarding house, but Charlie didn't seem too concerned. Then the back door swung open and three more men came in and sat down around the big table. Jackson recognized John Schultz, but he'd never seen the other two. Max Jensen and Eddy Slokum displayed that familiar woodsman look, and Jackson could only guess they were out-of-work sawyers.

All the men in the room except Charlie McCoy and Jackson seemed to know each other. Although Jackson had lived his whole life just fifteen miles away in La Crosse, he'd never been in West Salem before he started working for Abernathy, the same day McCoy had drifted into town. And they all knew why they were there; they had been recruited for their talents and resources, and they were all eager to get started. These men had some characteristics in common: they all had a desire to become wealthy, but they all lacked the ambition to engage in steady employment, and thus were all in a deplorable financial condition. That made the idea of a get-rich-quick scheme quite attractive to them all.

Joshua got up from the table and stepped over to the doorway into the barroom. He opened the door just a crack and peeked through. When he saw that all was quiet and his hired bartender had everything under control, he closed and bolted the door, and returned to his place at the table. "Okay, keep your voices low, boys," he said. "We don't want the whole damn town to know our plans."

With that said, Charlie picked up the deck of cards and laid out a number of cards in a line to simulate a train of railroad cars. Then he picked up two poker chips, placed them on the first card and pointed. "This is the locomotive. Engineer and fireman," he explained in a low tone. "When we get the train stopped, two of us will board the locomotive and take charge of the engineer and fireman."

"How do we get the train to stop?" Eddy asked.

"Somebody'll be on the track waving a red lantern. It'll be late at night... dark, so the engineer won't know why. He might think there's a bridge out, so he'll stop the train rather than taking a chance."

Everyone seemed to be in agreement that it would be easy enough to get the train stopped.

Then McCoy pointed to the second card, said "Tender... coal car," and then pointed to the next card in line. He reached into his pocket, pulled out a silver dollar and plunked it down on the third card. "This is where the fortune is, boys... the mail and express car, and a safe full o' money."

All eyes were focused on McCoy's little demonstration.

"That's where you come in, Schultz," McCoy went on. "I hear you're pretty handy with a stick of dynamite. Think ya can blow open a safe?"

"With my eyes closed," John Schultz replied.

"Good," McCoy said. "The rest of you will keep the passengers and crew intimidated by firing a few shots now and then. Joshua will supply the rifles." He nodded toward the gun rack on the wall across the room. Everyone glanced in the same direction. "And Louis has a stable full of horses. Anyone who doesn't have a horse, he'll furnish one."

"Where we gonna stop the train?" Eddy asked.

"Don't know for sure yet," McCoy said. "Prob'ly somewhere between Sparta and La Crosse. We'll do some scoutin' and find the right place."

"When?" Max asked quietly.

"Don't know that yet, either. There's a lot o' plannin' to do, and a lot of details to work out. Let's meet here again in a few days... say, Thursday night. And in the meantime, don't talk to nobody 'bout this... not even your families."

McCoy picked up his silver dollar. Everyone except Joshua and Louis left through the back door into the alley.

The next meeting of the gang did take place on Thursday night, and this time Jackson and Charlie McCoy were the first to arrive at the North Star Saloon. They'd had a great chicken stew supper at the boarding house after a long day of cutting more trees, so their bellies were full and Charlie especially was anxious to start laying the plans for his anticipated gain of wealth. He was already dreaming of his riches and visualizing himself basking in luxury, wearing silk shirts and alligator skin boots. He didn't plan to remain associated with any of the gang members once they had helped him pull off the heist, nor did he plan to stay in Wisconsin after this escapade. He could disappear into the population of New York or some other big city back east until the law had given up trying to solve the robbery. But he didn't mention any of this, even to Jackson, as he was sure it would cause some disloyalty among the gang members, and that would certainly decrease their chances of success.

When everyone had arrived, Joshua bolted the door to the barroom and took his seat at the big table. "Okay, boys," he said, taking command. "Anybody got any good ideas on where to stop the train?"

Several negative murmurs emitted from the group, and then Max Jensen spoke up. "Maybe at the long grade before the tunnel. It'd be going kinda slow there already."

Everybody mumbled a little and nodded heads, as if in agreement with the idea.

"But that would be too close to Tunnel City," said John Schultz. "If there's gonna be shootin' and there's damn well gonna be dynamite explodin'... too much noise. People at Tunnel City are bound to hear all that goin' on."

"Good point," Joshua commented. "But we'll keep it in mind as a possibility."

"It's about ten miles between Bangor and Sparta," Eddy said. "Bound to be someplace in that stretch."

"Could be," Louis Reed said. "But Rockland is right in the middle."

"Here's what we'll do, boys," Joshua cut in. "Who wants to do a little scouting? I'd bet Louis will supply the horses."

"Why, that's the best idea yet," said Charlie McCoy. "Me and Jackson can go out early Saturday morning. Hell... we can check it out, and we'll even figure out our escape route. I figure we should all split up... ride off in different directions, so there ain't no good trail for the law to follow, and then meet up somewhere a couple days later... to divvy up the loot."

"Mindoro would be a good place to meet up," Eddy offered.

"Too close," John argued. "Should be someplace farther

north… like Black River Falls."

Jackson just sat quietly listening to the less-than-agreeable conversation. It seemed as though everyone of the gang wanted to be in command. "We need a leader," he said. "Someone has to keep things organized."

"I agree with Jackson," said John Schultz. "And Joshua come up with the best ideas so far, about the scouting, so I think he should be the leader."

No one disputed John's suggestion, and everyone turned their eyes on Joshua, wondering if he would accept the appointment. He stared back at each one, realizing that they expected his approval, wanting him to accept the responsibility of organizing this bunch of unorganized characters.

"Okay," he finally said. "We're all in this together. I'll try to keep things in line."

Everyone seemed a little relieved, now that they had a leader. Even Charlie McCoy didn't object, even though this whole thing had been his idea in the first place, and he had always thought he would be the one calling the shots. But the others had looked to Joshua, perhaps because they knew him, and they were all aware that he possessed the intelligence to be a leader. But that was okay with McCoy, as it made his own private scheme easier to conceal from the others.

Chapter 13

J ackson was up early Saturday morning. He came downstairs to the dining room where Millie was setting the table and preparing to serve breakfast. McCoy had just come in too, and she seemed a bit startled as they entered the room. "My! You boys are up early," she said. "It's Saturday...you fixin' to go to work today?"

"No, ma'am," McCoy replied. "But we got someplace to go. We need some breakfast right away," he demanded.

Millie twisted her mouth in a sneer and glared at McCoy, and then at Jackson. She had always thought that it seemed a shame that such a nice boy as Jackson should be keeping company with a character like Charlie McCoy. To her, it just didn't seem right. "Well, sit down," she said reluctantly. "I'll see if the side pork is done fryin' and in the meantime, I'll bring in the hard-boiled eggs."

The two men gobbled down their breakfast and were long gone before any of the other boarders wandered down from their upstairs rooms. They were waiting with their bedrolls in hand at the livery stable when Louis Reed showed up.

It was that gray time of morning just before the sun broke over the hills in the east. The town was just waking up

"G-mornin' boys," Louis greeted them. "Ready to take a little ride?"

"Yeah," McCoy said. "Got a couple of good mounts for

us?"

Louis swung the big door open and pointed inside. "You can take Molly and Dan," he said. "Good saddle ponies." Then he led them to the harness room where they retrieved two saddles. When the horses were saddled and bridled, McCoy took the reins of the spotted gray mare named Molly, and Jackson prepared to mount the spirited roan steed named Dan.

"Now if anyone recognizes these horses and asks," Louis reminded them, "you're payin' two dollars a day."

McCoy tipped his hat and smiled a sinister grin. "Whatever you say. We should be back by sundown tomorrow."

They rode off toward the west. Their intentions were to inspect the entire route of the *Chicago Milwaukee & St. Paul* tracks from La Crosse to Tomah, and beyond if necessary. But in that distance they were certain they would find a good location to stop the train, do their dirty work, and have a safe escape route into the hills. McCoy's plan involved each gang member to ride off in different directions after the robbery. Then they would meet up again several days later, perhaps in another town.

The railroad tracks took a fairly straight course through the valley. The La Crosse River snaked its way through the broad valley, too, but its course was far from being straight. It was a splendid little river. It wasn't very long or wide like the great Mississippi that Jackson was used to, but it swelled big enough during the spring floods for the logging crews to float hundreds of thousands of pine logs downstream to the sawmills at La Crosse. That season was over now as the floodwaters had receded a week ago, and the La Crosse had returned to its near normal run of caramel-colored water. And now that the springtime fierceness and the log drives had left, deer and fox were returning to drink, and raccoons resumed their hunt for food, where the banks were abundant with frogs, and the shallows alive with fish.

Rich farmland lay on either side of the river, and gradually it was being stripped of trees making the land more useful for crops. The little river was dammed at a place called Neshonoc, where there had once been a town by that name, but the residents and businessmen had since moved to the new village of West Salem to be close to the railroad route on the other side of the valley. Now, all that was left at Neshonoc was the limestone gristmill and dam that held back the water to form a wonderful little lake. Spilling over the dam, the La Crosse tumbled over boulders and then wandered lazily through the oak and hickory and maple forests on its way to join the Mississippi.

They rode to within spitting distance from the La Crosse depot where they decided to stop a while and rest the horses. McCoy pulled out his pocket watch; it was nearly noon.

"Ya know," Jackson said. "Our house is only a half mile from here. Ma would be glad to cook us some dinner."

Charlie studied the surroundings as if he were planning an escape route if he needed one. Jackson waited patiently for his reply of approval.

"Not a good idea," Charlie finally said.

"Why not? You'll like my Ma's cooking?"

Charlie stared into Jackson's eyes. "And just how are you going to explain why we're here? You gonna tell her that we're out scoutin' to make plans for a train robbery?"

"Of course not. We'll just tell her we came out for a ride."

"Can't do it, Jack... can't take the chance on people seeing us here."

Jackson wanted to protest, but he thought better of it. He'd just play along with Charlie's lead.

"Besides," Charlie went on. "We got a lot of ground to cover today. We should get moving."

They rode back east, following the tracks this time instead of the wagon road. Charlie studied every foot of track and pondered all the surroundings as if he were calculating some complicated time and distance equation. Every time they heard a train coming from either direction, Charlie led them off into the trees where they would be out of sight, but could still watch the movement of the train. He studied the hills on either side of the valley, and submitted to memory the location of any farmhouses that were near the tracks. It made for slow progress, and by the time the sun was hovering just above the treetops to the west, they were only as far as Rockland. They headed for the general store, bought two cans of beans, a loaf of bread, a pound of smoked sausage, and a half-pound of beef jerky. They filled their canteens and rode off toward the towering mound of huge rocks just south of the little town.

"Is this where we camp for the night?" Jackson asked.

Charlie looked around. "No. I just wanna watch a train stop here at this depot," he said. "Then we'll move on... away from town somewhere."

After the next westbound train made its brief stop at the Rockland station, Charlie finally agreed to find a place to camp and eat. Jackson was starved.

About two miles east of town, the wagon road and

railroad tracks crossed in a clearing just beyond the edge of the woods. Charlie stopped and studied the surroundings for a couple of minutes. "Here," he said to Jackson. "This is where we'll camp... right at that tree line."

Jackson didn't need to be told twice. He galloped the roan to the trees, dismounted and immediately started gathering dry fallen branches to build a fire.

"This sure beats Kansas," Charlie said after the horses were unsaddled and tethered with long ropes so they could reach plenty of the hay grass out in the clearing.

"Why's that?" Jackson asked.

"Ain't no trees out there. Nothin' but buffalo chips to build a fire."

Jackson cut the lids off the bean cans with his knife and set them on a flat rock in the fire. "If there ain't no trees, what do they build houses with?"

"Sod. Most of the farm people build sod houses. Lumber has to be hauled in by wagon. 'Course, now the railroad hauls it in by the carload, and the farmers only have to haul it from Dodge City."

"You ever been to Dodge?"

"Sure. Drove cattle to the rail stockyards there many times."

"What's it like?"

"Well, Jack, it's beautiful. But next to Deadwood, it's the meanest city there ever were... saloons overflowin' with cattle drivers, road agents, prospectors, gunslingers, gamblers..." Charlie seemed to drift off into a dream. "... And lots of women... pretty ladies to sing and dance and lead you off to a room upstairs..." He remained in the trance. "With money in your pocket you can have anything a man could wish for."

Jackson tried to imagine the picture that Charlie was painting with words. He had always thought that La Crosse had everything a man could need, but Charlie was describing something more exciting, more adventurous, and certainly more dangerous for the average person. But it was clear to Jackson, now, that Charlie wasn't the average man, and he almost envied Charlie's adventurous spirit.

Darkness fell, and the little campfire twinkled bravely. They leaned back against their saddles on the ground and ate the beans and smoked sausage and bread.

"What's Deadwood like?" Jackson asked.

Charlie stared off into the night. "Well, Jack, it's meaner than Dodge, and a whole lot richer."

"Why is it meaner?"

"Well, for a long time there weren't no law. The Dakota Territory ain't part of the United States, and so people done pretty much whatever they wanted. The town was built with gold dug outa the hills, and with all that money around, and with no lawmen... well... a man could gun down another man for his gold and nothin' more was said. And the saloonkeepers and gambling house operators? They knew how to get the gold away from the miners that worked for it."

"You said you cut wood there?"

"Yeah, the first winter. Then after that I drove a freight wagon between there and Cheyenne."

Jackson was again intrigued with the stories Charlie went on to tell about killings in the streets, and shootouts between drunken gamblers, and stagecoach robbers. "I got to know the Collins gang—lived in the same house. They were a sad bunch..." Charlie told the whole story about the bungled stagecoach robberies, and then the train heists in Nebraska and how all of the gang had been captured or killed—all except one—Tom Nixon, who escaped to Canada and was never seen again.

Two trains had passed by, one eastbound and one westbound and Charlie had paused to study the trains as they rumbled along the rails.

Then, in the stillness of that cool spring night, a figure, indistinct and formless, wandered in the shadows. Charlie instinctively reached for his *Colt* revolver and was ready for the unexpected intrusion. Jackson held his breath.

And then the figure suddenly emerged from mystery into the clarity of the firelight. The visitor's horse nickered and the red firelight flashed on the silver bit and the shine of the polished saddle. The rider's face shone crimson at first, like a demon on the devil's mission, but as he neared, Jackson released his held breath with a sigh of relief. "Logan!" he called out. "What are you doin' out here?"

Logan pulled up the reins and Argo obediently stopped, but kept prancing in place for a few seconds. Seemingly surprised to hear Jackson's voice, Logan stared at the two dark figures just beyond the fire. "Jackson? Is that you?"

It was impossible to detect the redness on Jackson's face that would have been there even without the firelight. Although he was glad to see Logan instead of some stranger that he didn't trust, he knew it wasn't good that Logan should see him and Charlie together in the middle of the night, considering the reason for them being there. He had never told Charlie about his friendship with Logan, but now it appeared as though he would be required to come up with an explanation.

"Just passing through… on my way home," Logan replied. "What are *you* doing out here?"

"Aaaahhh, me 'n Charlie… we just went for a ride… campin' out."

"Okay," Logan said. "Well, I hope you got good warm blankets. Gonna be chilly tonight."

"We'll be okay," Jackson said.

"Okay. See ya 'round," Logan said, and he rode away into the darkness.

Charlie had noticed Logan's badge and had immediately holstered his pistol. "That was a lawman," he said to Jackson after the rider had disappeared. "You know him?"

"Yeah, I know him," the boy replied. "I talked to him the day I got off the train."

"Well, y' know, Jack," Charlie said with a sinister scowl. "You can't be rubbin' elbows with no lawman, understand?"

"Yeah, I understand." Jackson knew the reason for Charlie's dislike for having a deputy sheriff hanging around, but he certainly didn't want to end his friendship with Logan. He'd just have to keep it secretive.

After a while they rolled up in their blankets and went to sleep while a band of coyotes wailed like lost spirits.

THE GREAT TRAIN ROBBERY OF MONROE COUNTY

Chapter 14

J ackson woke up the next morning, rubbed his face with his hands and pulled on his hat. Charlie's blankets were rolled up and sitting about four feet from a small crackling fire.

The morning was sharply frostbitten and clear for as far as the eye could see. A lacy mist of fog rose from the water as if trying to hide the secrets of the river. Blackbirds cheered in the new day, and somewhere nearby a pair of squirrels scolded the blackbirds for making such a racket. The fresh smell of spring was in the air. Jackson loved this time of year.

"This is the place," Charlie said. He startled Jackson as he came from behind, out of the trees. In the distance they heard a whistle—a train approaching from Rockland.

"What d'ya mean?" Jackson asked.

"This is the perfect place to stop the train. Did you notice last night? The eastbound isn't moving very fast here. There are no houses anywhere around. I've been checking on that this morning. And there's good escape routes into the hills in every direction from here. It's perfect!"

The morning eastbound mail train rumbled past, a trail of black blowing from the engine's smokestack. Just as Charlie had commented, it wasn't rolling at top speed.

"It'll be easy enough for a couple of us to board the train at the Rockland depot when it's dark, and ride on the roof of the express car out to here..." Charlie continued to tell

Jackson his entire plan of jumping down onto the coal tender, making the engineer stop the train at gunpoint, and the other gang members would be waiting here in the woods. "Just like Jesse James used to do it," Charlie smiled. "And the James Gang never got caught robbin' trains."

To Jackson, Charlie seemed quite sure of himself, and he was right by saying that the James Gang hadn't been caught robbing trains. But the James Gang had a lot of practice, unlike the gang that Charlie and Joshua were leading here. But if this plan worked for the James Gang, then it should work just fine here, too.

They spent the rest of the day riding along the tracks all the way to the tunnel, but it seemed as though Charlie had made his choice, and he didn't show much interest in any other area.

As they rode back toward home, Charlie informed Jackson of another choice he had made. "Guess I'll be leavin' Abernathy," he said.

"You're quitting?"

"Yep. Can't be tied down no more."

"Well, Ed asked me the other day if I wanted to stay on... help him build fences this spring."

"Yeah, he asked me, too," Charlie said. "But I told him I had to be movin' on soon. And you'll be movin' on soon, too, y' know."

Late that afternoon they rode into West Salem. As they crossed Leonard Street on their way to return the horses to the livery barn, Logan cut them off. He'd been waiting and watching for Jackson, hoping for a social visit.

Jackson was just about to offer a friendly greeting when Charlie came between them and glared a stern "no" at him.

Jackson knew that Charlie meant business, and this was the right time to show Charlie that no friendship existed between him and Deputy Hans Logan.

"Hey, Deputy," Jackson sneered. He pointed up Leonard Street. "Isn't that a holdup goin' on? I think you better go stop it!"

Logan turned to look up Leonard Street toward the business section of town. It was Sunday, and nothing was going on. Leonard Street was nearly deserted. He turned back to Jackson, only to see menacing laughs coming from the two men on horseback as they rode away.

Jackson thought he'd given a good performance for Charlie. He looked rearward to see Logan riding in the opposite direction. He hoped that Logan would understand.

Chapter 15

A note was delivered to Jackson's room Monday evening after supper by Wendell, the less-than-bright boy that Joshua hired for such purposes. The note simply read:

Meeting tonight—9:00

The meeting slowly gathered in the back room of the North Star Saloon as usual. Jackson expected that this meeting was for the purpose of him and McCoy reporting their opinion on the best place for stopping the train. When everyone was present and Joshua had bolted the door, Charlie began his lecture of how the robbery was to unfold. "About two miles east of Rockland," he said, "The wagon road crosses the tracks."

"That would be Miller's Crossing," Max interrupted. "It's halfway between Rockland and Sparta."

Charlie continued with the entire plan, explaining where each man would be, and what he would do. "When Schultz blows open the safe and we get the loot out, we'll all ride in different directions. There's plenty of ways to get out of the valley from there. We'll decide where to meet up again at our next meeting," Charlie finished.

But before the discussions reached an end, another question of concern was brought up. "What if some of the crew recognizes us?"

"Kill 'em. Shoot 'em dead." A long moment of silence

lingered after Joshua rattled off the answer, as if he'd been waiting for someone to ask. The response nearly stopped Jackson from breathing. He glanced around the table at the others. Max and Eddy winced and looked down into the tabletop, hiding their expressions from the ringleaders.

Then Charlie spoke up. "It'll be dark as the bottom of a well at that time of night. And we'll all have our masks on. But we can't take any chances."

Jackson stepped out the back door of the saloon into the cool night. His head was spinning like a dog chasing its own tail. Words spoken at the meeting kept tumbling around in nightmarish fashion. Until now, he had thought of the pending train robbery as an exhilarating adventure and a chance for immediate riches. But now, there was talk about murder—killing innocent people for no reason. Taking money from the wealthy was one thing; taking lives was another.

Jackson knew he couldn't let this go on. At least he couldn't allow himself to be a part of it, and he even felt ashamed—guilt-ridden—that he had fallen into the temptations offered by a man he hardly knew.

He stumbled back to the Franklin Street boarding house and climbed the stairs, careful not to make any noise. He didn't want the other residents to know he had been out so late, stirring suspicions of his ill-doings.

Barely breathing for fear that someone might hear him, he lay still in bed, thoughts and visions tumbling about. And then another kind of fear engulfed him. It was then he realized the horror of reality: it would be impossible for him to just walk away from the gang. He knew their intentions, and in fact, every detail of their plans. If they were willing to kill innocent train passengers and crewmen to avoid the remote possibility of identification, they wouldn't hesitate to kill him if they thought he was being disloyal. He was caught in an evil trap from which there seemed no escape.

Then his visions focused on each gang member: Max and Eddy were just laborers at the Neshonoc Flourmill. They didn't seem to be the murderous type, and Jackson had caught a glimpse of them wincing a bit at the mention of killing if the need arose at the time of the holdup. Neither of them appeared much of a threat to him.

Louis Reed, the livery stable operator, as far as Jackson could tell, was a respected businessman in the town and hardly seemed the type to murder another human being, although he *was* Joshua Avery's partner and friend.

John Schultz, though, remained questionable. He always possessed that devilish, destructive look in his eyes. It probably was because of his love of dynamite and blowing things up. Whether or not that passion included people, Jackson couldn't be sure, but he thought not.

That left Joshua and Charlie. They were the ones Jackson feared most now. The saloon owner had come from Chicago, and although he treated his customers at the bar pleasantly, Jackson knew there was another side of Joshua that didn't surface to the eye of the public. Rumors that he had left Chicago because of his involvement with some sort of foul play were never confirmed. But Jackson didn't doubt the rumors were true. There seemed to be an undercurrent deep within his personality that carried an explosive temper that Jackson expected to erupt at any moment. And he had been the first to suggest killing anyone who appeared to recognize any one of the gang during the robbery.

Jackson stared out his window into the moonlit night. The image of Charlie McCoy loomed there in the black sky. Charlie had, as long as Jackson had known him, seemed to be his friend. They worked together, and they had always gotten along well. And Charlie had told him all those great stories about his life out in the West, about his acquaintances with some of the famous people—some of them outlaws— whom Jackson had read about in the newspaper. But now that he gave it serious thought, he wondered if it was more than just casual acquaintance.

Jackson had never considered himself a detective—he couldn't even find a missing sock in his own house. But this situation was becoming more serious than a missing sock, and it deserved some serious attention. Logan had taught him not to overlook the most obvious clues, and that sometimes happened with clues that were sitting right out in the open.

At that moment another vision abruptly appeared—the initials *T.N.* that were tooled on the expensive leather belt that Charlie always wore. He'd shrugged it off when Jackson asked what the letters stood for, and now he knew why. Charlie McCoy was not his real name. But who was he... really?

Jackson knew he wouldn't sleep another wink that night. He swung his feet over the edge of the bed and sat up. It was chilly outside, but not so bad as to be uncomfortable if he dressed for it. He slipped on his trousers, socks, and a wool shirt. With boots and hat in hand he quietly padded down the hallway and then down the stairs. He would pull on his boots after he got out on the porch, and maybe no one in the house would hear him leaving.

It didn't seem as cold now as it had earlier when he left the saloon. But his thoughts didn't linger very long on the weather. He had more important things to consider now. Somehow he thought for certain that his own safety was in jeopardy. A long walk out into the country would help him think this predicament through. He headed for the river.

Top priority was trying to figure out who Charlie really was, and why he would want to hide his real identity. It had seemed that he had arrived in town on his last Double Eagle. But the more Jackson thought about that, Charlie had never once seemed concerned about money, and he always seemed to have plenty of it when they visited the North Star. In fact, he always seemed to have a twenty-dollar gold piece readily available. Perhaps this wasn't his first train holdup.

The initials on the belt came to mind again as Jackson walked slowly along the riverbank. Charlie had talked about all the people he knew in Deadwood: Wild Bill Hickok, although it had been for only a few days until he was gunned down in a gambling hall; Wyatt Earp had even spent one winter there, but Deadwood's Sheriff Seth Bullock had sort of run him out of town. Mostly, though, Charlie talked about a particular gang—the Collins Gang—that had been involved in stagecoach holdups, and then ventured to Nebraska to rob a train. He had lived in the same house with them in Deadwood, and perhaps that was why he knew so many details. "Let's see," Jackson said aloud, knowing there was no one around to hear him. "There was Joel Collins, and Sam Bass, and Jack Davis…"

He stopped and stared at the far riverbank, clearly visible in the bright moonlight. His thoughts were dredging up more names, and the stories connected with them. He'd heard so much about these guys in Deadwood that he felt like he almost knew them himself. "And there was Robert McKimie, and Bill Heffridge, and Jim Berry, and... and... and *Tom Nixon.*

Now the final story of the Collins Gang raced through Jackson's head. *Jim Berry and Tom Nixon left together each with their share of the money—ten thousand dollars in newly minted twenty-dollar gold pieces. Nixon told Berry he was headed to Florida and they split up. But when they were a safe distance apart, Nixon had turned northward to Canada and was never heard from or seen again.*

"Now if they were the only ones there, and if they split up, how could Charlie... *or anyone,* for that matter... know that Nixon turned north to Canada?"

Jackson stood absolutely still as he continued to stare across the river. "T. N." he said softly, and then he repeated it several times. "He couldn't know that... unless he was there... and he *was there...* he's *Tom Nixon...* T. N."

He had covered his trail, all right. So well, in fact, that even the Pinkertons had lost track of him, and had obviously given up their search. And after this long—six or seven years—they probably had little or no interest in him.

Jackson knew he had to find a way to stop the gang's plan to rob the train and perhaps killing innocent people. He had quite certainly stumbled onto a seasoned outlaw; one he had been working alongside all winter and never realized that he was a hardened criminal capable of not only robbery, but hurting and even killing other people. And quite obviously, he was an accomplished liar. Charlie—*or Tom*—had made everyone here believe he was Charlie McCoy, an ordinary drifter looking for work. But in reality, he was a highly-skilled con man who had kept the law and even the Pinkertons at bay for many years.

Jackson needed to find his good friend Hans Logan. Logan would know what to do at a time like this. But Jackson hadn't made this part easy: not long ago, he had acted against his better judgment in severely damaging his relationship with Logan. Logan hadn't been around to see him since, and he wondered if there was any hope of salvaging their friendship.

Chapter 16

I t was nearly two o'clock in the morning. This probably wasn't a good time to go knocking on Logan's door, but such a matter couldn't wait. What Charlie McCoy and his gang were planning had to be stopped, and Logan was the only person who would be likely to listen. At least, Jackson hoped he would listen. And when he gave all this valuable information to the deputy, perhaps it would be enough to make Logan forget about their differences, and they could be friends again, like they had started out.

Jackson didn't waste any more time thinking about what he had to do. He quickly turned and started up along the river. He was thankful that the night sky was clear and the moon shone brightly, lighting his way, so crossing the river on the rocks below the dam at McMillan's flourmill wouldn't be quite so treacherous. Logan's farm was just around the hill from the dam.

As he cautiously jumped from boulder to boulder with the La Crosse River just inches below him, he thought about how he would try to get Logan awake at two in the morning. He wasn't much in favor of knocking on the front door and waking the whole family. But he knew where Logan's bedroom window was located at the rear of the house. He gathered a few small pebbles from the riverbank.

Plink.

Plink, plink.

The first pebbles on Logan's second story window pane

didn't seem to gain any results.

Plink, plink.

Plink, plink.

Jackson thought he saw movement in the darkened window, and then the sash slowly slid upward. The room behind it was still dark, and Jackson could only hear the loud whisper say "Who's out there?"

"Logan," Jackson answered with a loud whisper. "It's me, Jackson."

There was a long pause, and then he saw a face appear as Logan leaned out the window for a better look at the shadowy figure below him.

"What are you doing here?" Logan asked with a disgusted tone. "It's two o'clock in the morning."

"I know. But this is important," Jackson said.

"If this is just another one of your foolish pranks," Logan replied, "then just go away." He pulled back inside the window so Jackson could no longer see him.

"NO! Wait!" Jackson pleaded. "It's no joke. It's serious."

There was no reply from the second story window. Just silent darkness.

Jackson wasn't sure if Logan was even listening now, but he knew he had to try to get Logan to hear him out, even if he couldn't make him understand that their friendship was still important. "I'm sorry, Logan, that I sorta ruined our friendship. But I hope I can make you understand that it wasn't all my idea." His voice was quivering, almost to the point of sobbing. "I made a big mistake, Logan. Please... trust me."

There was still no response from the window.

"You see... I got hitched up with the wrong people. I

know that now, and I need your help."

He stared up at the dark, empty window.

"They're apt to kill me if they find out I'm here talking to you." He was hoping that remark would draw Logan back out, but it did not.

"Logan, please... you've got to listen to me. There's gonna be a train robbery. Innocent people might get shot."

In the next instant, Logan's face once again appeared as he leaned out the window. Relief flowed through Jackson's entire body. Logan *was* listening.

"What did you say?" Logan asked.

"There's... there's gonna be a train hold-up."

"How d'ya know that?"

"'Cause I've been ridin' with the gang that's gonna pull it off... that's how I know."

"Jackson... wait right there. I'll be down in a minute." Logan closed the window and Jackson stood there in silence, shivering from fear of what he had just done. He was thoroughly convinced that Charlie McCoy and Joshua Avery would not hesitate to kill him, now that he was about to reveal to the law their plan to murder and steal. For a few moments he thought of just running away, before he said any more to Logan. But that would be the cowardly way out, and it certainly wouldn't mend a broken friendship that he so desperately wanted to fix.

A couple of minutes passed and Jackson heard a door open and footsteps fall across the front porch. Then Logan slowly emerged from the shadow of the house cast by the bright moonlight, but he stopped ten feet short of reaching Jackson, as if he were sensing danger and exercising extreme caution. He was only half dressed—jeans pulled over a nightshirt, pants legs neither inside nor outside of his boots, and his sandy blond hair in a tangled mess without a hat covering it.

"You don't have your gun," Jackson whispered loud enough for Logan to hear.

"No... didn't think I'd need it."

"But I could be a dangerous criminal."

"You *could be*, but you're not. You're Jackson."

Jackson stepped closer. "I'm... I'm really sorry about what happened before."

"And you came all the way out here to throw rocks at my window and wake me up in the middle of the night to tell me?"

"No... well, yeah... but there's more to it than that. I never meant no harm. See, it was Charlie who said I couldn't be rubbin' shoulders with no lawman. It just wouldn't be right. So I couldn't let him know that we was friends."

Logan stepped closer now. "Wouldn't be right for what?"

"Well... that's what I gotta talk to you about."

Just then another second-story window slid open and the elder Logan leaned out. "Everything okay, Hans? Is there trouble?"

"No, Pa. Everything's fine. It's just my friend Jackson. We're gonna go out to the barn to talk. Go back to bed." Then he grabbed Jackson's arm and started leading him off into the darkness behind the house. When they reached the barn door, Logan unlatched it, swung it open, stepped inside and lit a lantern hanging on the wall. Then he pulled Jackson inside and closed the door. He sat down on a pile of hay and looked up into Jackson's eyes. "Okay... so what's this all about?"

Jackson was a little taken by the abruptness of Logan's actions. "Does this mean we're still friends?"

"Yes... of course... unless you're gonna tell me otherwise."

Jackson cautiously sat in the hay beside Logan. "Well," he said, hesitating. "There's a lot to tell."

"Well," Logan replied, staring his friend in the eyes. "Let's hear it."

"Okay... for starters, Charlie McCoy isn't his real name. His real name is Tom Nixon... who was a member of the Collins gang out in Deadwood... in the Dakota Territory."

Logan rubbed his chin with his fingertips. "The Collins gang," he said thoughtfully. "Didn't they get caught out in Nebraska? Or was it Kansas?"

"They did," said Jackson. "All but one... Tom Nixon. He got away and headed to Canada with his share of the money they stole from a train. Ten thousand dollars."

"And how do you know Charlie is this Tom Nixon?"

"I figured that out just a little while ago. He told me the story about the train robbery in Nebraska, and how the gang split up and headed in different directions. If Tom Nixon was riding all alone, and there was no one else there, how could he *possibly* know that Tom Nixon turned north and went to Canada and was never heard of again? And it kinda explains why he wears a belt with the initials TN on the back."

"Hmmm." Logan scratched his chin some more. "Guess I never noticed his belt." He got up off the hay and walked to the stall where Argo spent his nights, and right next to him was Apollo. He rested his elbows on the top of the stall, gazing at his noble horse.

Jackson rose to his feet, watching Logan, and thinking that Logan had become disinterested. "You could check it out, couldn't you? I mean, through the Sheriff's office, you could..."

"Sure," Logan said. "I'll have the sheriff send a telegram to Deadwood."

"The sheriff's name there is Seth Bullock... or at least that's what Charlie told me."

"Okay... now what's this you said about there's gonna be a train robbery?"

Jackson leaned on the stall beside Logan. "One day while me and Charlie were out cuttin' trees on Abernathy's place, Charlie said I could be rich if I helped him rob a train."

Logan gave him a startled glare. "And you agreed? Just like that?"

"I thought he was joking at first. But then he kept on about it, saying how easy it was, and how we'd never get caught, and how rich we'd be. I guess the thought of being rich got the best of me, and the next thing I knew I was in the middle of a gang that was planning a train robbery."

"What train? When? Where?"

"I think the Milwaukee 'n St. Paul. Someplace between the tunnel and La Crosse, but they haven't decided when."

"Who's in this gang besides you and Charlie McCoy?"

"Well the leader is Joshua Avery."

Logan's eyes widened. "The owner of the North Star?"

"Yeah. We have all our meetings in the back room. Him and Charlie seem to be the ones making all the decisions. When they started talking about killing people on the train during the holdup... well... that's when I decided I should get out. But now they'll kill *me* if I quit, 'cause I know all their plans."

"Who else comes to the meetings?"

"Well, there's John Schultz... he's the dynamite expert."

"Dynamite! What the hell..."

"To blow open the safe in the express car," Jackson explained. "That's where the big money is. And Louis Reed is..."

"Louis? At the livery stable?"

"Yeah. He's supplying the horses. And then there's Max Jensen and Eddy Slokum."

"Max and Eddy! Why, they're just a couple of workers at McMillan's mill. How do they fit in?"

"They're s'posed to be good with rifles."

"Anybody else?"

"No. That's all I know of. Logan? I'm scared. I don't know what to do. They'll kill me if I run out now."

Logan put his arm around Jackson's shoulders. "Showing your fear to them now is what will get you in trouble." He guided Jackson back to the hay pile and they sat down. "Here's what we'll do," he went on. "You just keep playing along with whatever they do, and don't let on that you're gonna quit on 'em. I'll talk to the sheriff... and I'll make sure he understands that you're on our side. Okay?"

Jackson nodded.

"I'll get the sheriff to send off some telegrams... try to find out more about Tom Nixon. In the meantime, you learn all you can about the robbery plans. We'll meet again when you find out when and where. Okay?"

"Okay. But how are we gonna meet again? I can't let them see me talking to you."

"Do they know you're here tonight?"

"I don't think so."

"Then we'll meet the same way. You toss a stone at my window to wake me."

Chapter 17

T he sun was barely peeking over the hills when Logan galloped Argo into Sparta. He dashed quickly into Sheriff Colby's office, determined to be the first to get the sheriff's attention. He sat at a table writing down notes of all that Jackson had told him in the wee hours of the morning when the sheriff walked in.

"Well, good morning Logan," the sheriff said with a smile. "You're here mighty early today."

"Morning, Sheriff. I got something really important to tell you about."

"Can it wait 'til this afternoon?" Colby said as he sat down behind his desk. "I've got a lot of paperwork to catch up on."

"No, sir," the deputy replied. "This is really important and it can't wait."

"Well, okay, then. But be quick about it."

"Thank you, sir." Logan pulled his chair in front of the sheriff's desk. "I have learned about a train robbery that is going to take place in this county."

"A train robbery!" Sheriff Colby beamed with a bigger grin. "You certainly must be joking. Who would rob a train in this part of the country?"

"Well, Sheriff, there is a gang formed over in West Salem that's planning on robbing a train."

Colby's expression turned solemn. "You sound serious

about this. How did you learn of this plan?"

"From one of the gang members."

"From one of them? He just came right out and told you they were going to rob a train?"

"Well, sort of. He threw rocks at my bedroom window in the middle of the night and woke me."

Sheriff Colby squinted and leaned forward a little.

"Yes, sir. You see, he's a good friend of mine and I trust what he told me is true."

The sheriff's eyes widened. "Logan! A good friend of yours is a member of a gang planning a train robbery? I thought you chose your friends a little more carefully."

"Please... let me explain. His name is Jackson Evans. He's only seventeen years old, from La Crosse, working for Ed Abernathy cutting trees off his cropland."

Colby leaned back in his chair. "Go on, Logan. I'm listening."

"Jackson is not a bad person. He mistakenly got caught up in this gang because of the other woodcutter Abernathy hired... a drifter who came through here about the time Ed was hiring. I talked to him last fall... when he first came into town. Gave his name as Charlie McCoy."

"So, this McCoy is the leader of the gang?"

"Him and Joshua Avery, the owner of the North Star Saloon in West Salem."

"Joshua Avery came from Chicago about a year ago," the sheriff said. "Doesn't surprise me... all these big city folk coming in here and causing trouble."

"Yes, well, I just want you to understand that Jackson Evans is on our side. He's gonna keep meeting with the gang and learn as much as he can about when and where. Then he'll secretly let me know."

"Oh! So, you have a spy!"

"Yes, sir. I guess you could call him that."

"Well, you should have him come and talk to me."

"No, he won't do that."

"Why not?"

"He's afraid McCoy and Avery will kill him if they find out he's turned against them."

"Yes, well, I guess that's a good enough reason to stay away from the Sheriff's Office. Just how is he going to inform you?"

"Oh, he'll throw stones at my window again."

Colby lifted an eyebrow. "Are you sure this isn't just some kid's prank?"

"Yes, sir, I'm sure. And there's one more thing."

"What is it?"

"Charlie McCoy is a fake name. There's good reason to believe that his name is really Tom Nixon. He was a member of the Collins Gang. If I remember correctly, they were caught for train robbery in Nebraska in 1878 or '79. But Nixon got away, and now he's here."

"How do you know all this?"

"I have a very clever spy," Logan replied with a grin. "Can you telegraph the sheriff in Deadwood, out in Dakota Territory? I'd feel better if we verified the story."

"I have a better idea," Colby said. "You know all the information. You go to the telegraph office and send the wire. Sign my name to it... the sheriff out there is more apt to answer it if it comes from another sheriff."

"Thank you, Sheriff. I'll do it right away."

The next morning Logan was surprised with a reply telegraph from Sheriff Seth Bullock, Deadwood, Dakota Territory. It had been delivered to Sheriff Colby by a messenger from the railroad telegraph office. There seemed to be little faith that Nixon had been discovered, but the telegram verified that everything Jackson had heard from McCoy was true. All of the Collins gang had been captured or killed by lawmen—all except Tom Nixon who had simply disappeared. He was still wanted by the Pinkerton Agency and just about every sheriff in Nebraska, not to mention the Union Pacific Railroad. But little hope remained of ever finding him or recovering the railroad's money. Even the Pinkertons had all but given up their search.

Logan was anxious to tell Jackson about the telegram, but he knew he had to wait for Jackson to come to him in the cover of darkness and in the privacy of his own barn.

Chapter 18

Sheriff Colby stepped out of his office to see Deputy George Clark by the front door.

"Mornin' Sheriff."

"Good morning, George. Where's Sam?"

"Should be on his way here right now. He was having breakfast over at the hotel."

"Okay. I want you two in my office when he gets here."

Behind a closed door, Colby explained the situation as he knew it to his two deputies, George Clark and Sam Gorman: "Seems that young Logan has stumbled onto something. There's a man in West Salem working for Ed Abernathy using the name Charlie McCoy as an alias. His real name is Tom Nixon; he's wanted by the Nebraska authorities, the Union Pacific Railroad, and the Pinkertons."

"What's he wanted for?"

"Train robbery." Colby handed the telegram to the deputies.

"You want us to bring him in?"

"No. Not yet. You see, he's fixin' to rob another train... right here in this county. I'll... er... we'll be famous when I... I mean... we... capture him and his gang red-handed."

"How are we gonna be able to do that?"

"Young Logan has an informant—some kid that's a member of the gang. He'll tell Logan when and where. Then we can be ready and waiting for them."

"So, I suppose," said George. "The kid gets some sort of special treatment."

"Special treatment?" the sheriff responded with a sneer. "Sure. He's the first one you should shoot for trying to get away."

The deputies frowned and shot an unfavorable glare at Colby.

"C'mon, boys. You don't want some kid taking credit and ruin our day of glory for rounding up a gang of desperados, do you?"

"What about Logan? Sounds like he's the one who deserves the credit."

The sheriff pondered on that for a moment. "Don't worry. I'll find a way to keep him out of it, too."

Colby hadn't yet done anything noteworthy as sheriff. He realized he could gain a little fame and recognition for arresting a noted outlaw like Tom Nixon, and why not make it happen in some spectacular way? And there could be nothing more spectacular than catching an outlaw in the middle of a train robbery. He would become a hero and a legend in his own time! And it was clear that he didn't particularly want to share the commendation with anyone.

Chapter 19

"Okay, boys," Joshua Avery said to open the late night meeting in the locked back room of the North Star. "I have some good news."

Everyone around the table perked up. Jackson was doing his best not to let his fear show. He had a job to do, and it was going to be his best effort to make certain these crooks would get caught before they had an opportunity to hurt anyone. He made himself look eager to take part in the plan.

"My good friend in Chicago has informed me that there will be a westbound train carrying seventy-five thousand dollars in the express car bound for La Crosse this Friday night. It's the payroll money for the lumber companies... the loggers that were in the north woods all winter."

"That is, my friends," Charlie McCoy chimed in, "... a little over ten thousand for each of us."

Renewed enthusiasm gushed into the room. The sound of that much money spurred a generous jolt of encouragement.

"Now," Joshua continued. "That train will be coming

through here a little after ten at night. Because of the good scouting done by Charlie and Jackson, we've come up with the perfect plan."

Jackson didn't care how perfect their plan was. He was even more determined, now, because the money they planned to steal was the money that would pay his father's wages for a long hard winter in the Chippewa River Valley, far away from his home and family, living in deplorable conditions and contending with the brutal weather. His family needed that money to survive, and under no circumstances was Jackson going to allow these men to deprive them of it.

"At ten-fifteen, the westbound will pull into the Rockland Depot," Charlie explained. "There is very little going on in Rockland at that time of night, and rarely if ever are any passengers getting on or off the train there. The train stops only to drop off and pick up mail, so there won't be anyone around except the depot agent. The rest of the town will be sound asleep. We'll make our strike there."

"Right at the depot?" Max asked. "Isn't that a little risky?"

"Actually, no," Joshua replied. "Passengers and conductors will not be alarmed by a regular stop, so no one will be concerned."

"Okay. I guess that makes sense."

Charlie went on. "You'll all meet at nine o'clock at the big rocks. It'll be dark by then and no one will notice you gathering there. You'll have a couple extra saddled horses with you. Me and Schultz will already be on the train. We'll get on at Sparta to make sure it stops in Rockland to let us off. A few minutes past ten, you'll quietly walk to the depot...

and make sure you have your masks on."

Joshua took over. "Me and Louis will go inside and take care of the agent. Once we have him tied and gagged, and smash the telegraph key, it'll only take one to guard him. Jackson—you can do that.

"Max and Eddy will take a stand at each end of the depot and watch for any trouble. If anything happens, come out shooting. When the train is stopped, Louis and me will jump aboard the engine and take charge of the engineer and fireman. When the express agent opens the door of the express car to exchange mail bags, Charlie and Schultz will jump him, get into the express car, blow open the safe, and grab the loot. When they've got the money off the train, we'll make the engineer pull the train out of the station."

"Then," Charlie said, "We all meet back at the rocks, get our horses and ride for the hills. Everybody head in different directions so there won't be a good trail for the law to follow. Saturday night, after dark, we'll meet in a little town called Hillsboro southeast of here. We'll split up the money, and then everyone is on his own. Any questions?"

"Who's gonna be carryin' all the money to Hillsboro?" Eddy asked.

"Me and Schultz," Charlie replied.

"And just how are we gonna find you in Hillsboro?"

"There's a saloon. We'll meet there."

"And just how do we *know* you're gonna be there?"

"You all have my word... *we'll be there*," Charlie said. Then he glared at John Schultz with a stern eye. "Schultz?"

"Oh, yeah," John agreed. "We'll be there!"

"Why don't we just divide up the money at the rocks?" Max inquired with a suspicious tone.

"There won't be time. We'll want to get away from Rockland as soon as we can... before someone comes to investigate the explosion. Somebody's bound to hear the dynamite."

Chapter 20

J ackson knew he couldn't just go to Logan's place right away. If any of the other gang members saw him heading in that direction instead of toward the boarding house, they might get suspicious. So when the others decided to go into the barroom and have a drink to celebrate their forthcoming wealth, he said he just wanted to go home to bed.

"Jackson, you have to come and have a drink with us," Charlie insisted. He wrapped a strong arm around the boy's shoulders and guided him into the bar. "We have to seal our oath of honor with whiskey!"

The saloon had closed long ago; all the patrons had left and only Willy, the hired bartender was there washing glasses and wiping down the bar. Most of the lights had been turned off and just a few gas lamps dimly lit the barroom.

"Go on home, Willy," Joshua said. "I'll take care of the rest."

So Willy gladly untied his apron and tossed it under the bar. Joshua escorted him to the front door. "Good night, Willy," he said, patting him on the shoulder. "Say hello to your lovely wife for me, and I'll see you tomorrow night." He locked the door behind Willy and went behind the bar. Then he set out seven glasses and poured from a bottle of his finest whiskey. He picked up one of the glasses and raised it in the air. "Drink up, boys! Here's to our new fortune!"

Knowing the entire place was empty except for them, they all let loose with whoops and cheers, and each gulped down the whiskey. Jackson was afraid to show any reluctance; he pretended to be as joyous as the others. He'd never drunk whiskey before—only beer and ale, and on occasion a little brandy. He sipped at the fiery drink, and then finally threw down the last swallow. It instantly warmed his insides after it left a burning trail down his throat. His eyes widened a little with shock, and he felt as though he was about to breath fire. But the others were obviously not paying much attention to him and in the dim light didn't notice his reaction to his first experience with whiskey.

Now that he thought he had met his obligation with one drink, he would hurry back to the boarding house, and then sneak over to Logan's place to deliver the information. He would betray the others, but he knew it was true: there is no honor among thieves.

Charlie, however, was not making it easy for him to leave the party. Holding firmly onto his shoulder and forcing another glass of whiskey in his hand, he said, "Just think, Jackson. In a couple of days we'll be rich. Have another drink to celebrate."

Jackson could only force a smile and take the drink. And after a couple more, his vision was getting a little fuzzy and his sense of balance was minimal. "Ch-Charlie," he slurred. "I haffa go home. I'm... awful... tired."

Charlie laughed. "You're awful drunk... that's your problem." He guided Jackson to the door and helped him out into the street. "Can you make it back to the boarding house okay?"

"Shhhhhhure... whish way is it?"

Charlie pointed him in the right direction and he staggered down Leonard Street. When he reached Franklin and turned the corner, he knew he was out of sight from Charlie... if Charlie was even watching. He straightened himself up from the staggering slouch and leaned against a maple tree. He was proud of the act he had used to get away, but the affects of the whiskey were still quite real. He took a deep breath and tried to relax. After a few moments he remembered that he had to get to Logan's place on the other side of the river, but it wasn't clear to him why. "Oh, yeah," he giggled. "I haffa tell Logan that we're gonna rob a train."

He desperately tried to shake off the stupor and concentrated on every step he took toward the river. It seemed much farther this night than it ever had before. When he finally reached the riverbank, he looked both ways, trying to determine which way it was to the dam. "That way," he said, pointing upstream. He stumbled along the bank until he reached the shallow water just below the dam where he could cross on the rocks. The sound of water rushing through the sluice gate at the dam seemed much louder than usual, and for good reason. The water level was high and the gate had been opened more. That meant the water below the dam would be a little deeper and the rocks a little harder to find. But he had to try. He had to get to Logan.

The first few boulders appeared quite distinctly in the blackness that engulfed everything, and the water sparkled here and there from the starlight. Jackson wished there were a bright moon to light his way, but it was merely a sliver, and a few pesky clouds kept it covered most of the time. But the rocks were there, he knew, and just a little caution would get him across the river. But the sight of swirling water below his feet didn't combine well his spinning head. Dizziness started to overcome and he began stepping more quickly to reach the other bank before total loss of balance would...

Too late. He hit the cold water with a spectacular splash. Fortunately for Jackson, it was only knee deep. Scrambling to his feet, the iciness rendered its sobering effect, and he sloshed his way to the far bank, and then continued on the rest of the journey around the hill to Logan's place. Unfortunately, the sobering effect of the fall into the chilly river wasn't lasting, and by the time Jackson arrived at Logan's house, the whiskey once again commanded his head. Two windows now occupied the upper wall of the rear of the house where only one had been before. He closed one eye, and miraculously one window disappeared. When he felt the relief of conquering that obstacle, he abruptly realized that he had forgotten to pick up some small stones at the riverbank. Dropping to his knees he groped through the grass hoping to find something he could fling at Logan's window. Luckily, his sense of touch wasn't impaired quite as bad as his vision—he found four small stones. Still a little shaky, he stood up, closed one eye and took aim at the window. The first rock clunked against the wall, missing its mark by at least four feet. The second, third and fourth tries weren't much better, but the noise had awakened Logan anyway. He went to the window, opened it and peered down at Jackson. It was rather dark, but he thought Jackson's clothes looked wet. His hat was gone and his hair seemed all pasted down. "Why are you all wet?" he asked in a loud whisper.

"I guesh I fell in the river."

"Wait right there. I'll be right down."

Logan quickly slipped on his jeans and boots, and then

hurried down to the back yard where Jackson stood shivering.

"Why did you fall in the river?"

"I... I had... a lill... too mush whishkey... at the shaloon... and I guesh I losh my balanch on the rocks."

Logan instantly recognized the problem. He steadied Jackson with his arm around his friend while he guided him to the barn. Inside, he sat Jackson down on a pile of hay and lit a lantern. "You're lucky you didn't drown," he said as he started unbuttoning Jackson's shirt. When they had removed all the wet clothes, Logan found a horse blanket and wrapped it around Jackson.

"Stay right here," he said. "I'll be right back with some dry clothes." He ran out of the barn, and a few minutes later he returned with a dry shirt and jeans. But by that time, Jackson had laid down and fallen asleep. Logan knew that he had come with information about the train robbery plans, but how he had gotten into this condition was likely the work of Charlie and the rest of the gang. The only thing to do now was to let Jackson sleep it off. But he couldn't just leave him there alone, so Logan decided to stay there with him all night until he woke up in the morning. He curled up in the hay with another horse blanket. Sleep didn't come easy.

Chapter 21

Logan had dumped a bucket of oats in the feed boxes for Argo and Apollo, and he was combing Argo's mane when Jackson threw back the blanket, stood up and said, "Where am I?" It was then he realized he was completely naked. He looked curiously at Logan, and then it seemed as if some of the details were creeping out of the shadows. He stood there, thinking of running somewhere to hide, but that seemed a little foolish. "Okay. So where are my clothes?" he asked Logan.

"They're out on Ma's clothesline. Don't think they're dry yet, but here's some of mine you can use in the meantime," Logan said as he handed Jackson the shirt and jeans.

"Dry?"

"Don't you remember falling in the river last night on your way here?"

Jackson's eyes narrowed to just slits and his brow wrinkled in deep thought. "Oh... yeah... I guess I do," he said as he started pulling on the jeans. "But how did..." he looked back at the blanket on the hay, and then back at Logan.

"You woke me up in the middle of the night... remember? Then we came to the barn and I went to get you some dry clothes, but you fell asleep before I came back. So I just let you sleep."

Jackson sat down on the hay again, the shirt draped across his legs. He put his elbows on his knees and propped his forehead in his hands. It was all coming back to him, how after the gang meeting Charlie had gotten him drunk on whiskey. And then he'd fallen in the river trying to get here. It was all a little embarrassing, and he was thankful Logan had found him and not someone else.

"I didn't tell you anything about the train robbery, did I?"

"No," Logan said. He sat down on the hay beside Jackson.

Jackson's eyes widened and he snapped his head up. "What day is it?"

"Thursday," Logan replied.

"Tomorrow! They're gonna rob the train Friday night!"

"Okay," Logan said. "Calm down and tell me all about it."

Jackson took a deep breath. "Last night at the North Star we had a meeting. Joshua and Charlie laid out the whole plan. And d'ya know what, Logan? D'ya know what?"

"Wh-what?"

"There's gonna be seventy-five thousand dollars on that train! And d'ya know what that money is for? Huh? Do ya?"

"No. What?"

"It's the payroll money for the logging companies! Part of that money belongs to my dad! You can't let them steal my dad's money!"

Logan put his arm across Jackson's shoulders. "Now calm down, Jackson. We're not gonna let anything of the sort happen. You just have to tell me what the plan is so we can stop them. Okay?"

Jackson took another deep breath. "Okay."

"Now, where is the robbery going to happen?"

"At the Rockland depot. We're all s'posed to meet at the big rocks at nine o'clock tomorrow night."

"They're gonna hold up the train at the depot?"

"Yeah. At 10:15 when the train pulls into the depot..."

Jackson went on to tell Logan the entire robbery plan while Logan listened intently. "...And then Charlie said he and John Schultz would meet the rest of us at the saloon in Hillsboro Saturday night to split up the money."

"Okay," Logan said. "Have you told me everything?"

"Everything I can remember."

"Well, then, put your shirt on and let's see if Ma will make us some breakfast."

Chapter 22

When they had eaten their breakfast and Logan sent Jackson on his way back to the boarding house, he saddled Argo and rode for Sparta. It would be mid-morning by the time he got there, and the sheriff would probably be in his office taking care of paperwork. Clouds were rolling in from the west; it looked like rain was on the way.

"Sheriff... I have news about the train hold-up."

"Well, then come right in and sit down," Colby said.

Logan sat down in front of the sheriff's desk; for some reason he felt uneasy about Colby's eagerness. "I spoke with Jackson. He gave me the whole plan."

"Good! Good! Let's hear it."

"Well, sir, they plan to strike the 10:15 arrival in Rockland... when it pulls into the station."

The sheriff's beaming smile turned a little sour. "Rockland! Why, that's not..."

"Not in this county," Logan said. "Perhaps we should contact the La Crosse County sheriff."

"No. I... we... can handle this. Go on, Logan."

"There will be a large sum of money in the express car... payroll for the logging companies. John Schultz, one of the gang members, is a dynamite expert. They're going to blow the safe when the train stops in Rockland. Two of the men will already have captured and tied the station agent before the train arrives, and then they will take control of the engineer and fireman while McCoy and Schultz enter the express car. Once the safe is blown open and they get the money, they'll send the train on its way and make their getaway on horses hidden at the rocks. Then they plan on meeting in Hillsboro Saturday night to split up the money."

Colby leaned back in his chair. "How many did you say they were?"

"Seven, counting Jackson."

"That's your young informant friend?"

"Yes sir."

"And what did you tell him to do this morning?"

"I told him, no matter what, to play along with everything the gang was doing in preparation, so they don't suspect that anybody's onto them."

"Good, boy, Logan. You did just fine. I think me and some deputies will be boarding that train here in Sparta. We'll have a little surprise waiting for them."

"Oh! But Sheriff... two of their men are boarding the train in Sparta... McCoy and Schultz. They'll recognize you for sure. You'll scare them off."

"Ah, you're probably right," Colby agreed. He scratched his chin. "Then we'll ride to Tunnel City earlier and board there."

"Promise me one thing, Sheriff."

"What's that?"

"That you'll tell all our men not to hurt Jackson. He's a good person, and he's the only reason we're gonna catch these outlaws."

"I'll see what I can do. Now go round up as many of our special deputies as you can find. Have them come here this afternoon for a little meeting at one o'clock."

"Okay, Sheriff. Will do."

Chapter 23

L ogan knew where to find most of the special deputies—those who were called to duty only when the need arose. He hoped he would get to them all, and then get Argo into City Livery before the rain came; he hated to make Argo stand out in the rain.

His first stop would be at E. Thorbus & Son, the largest agricultural machinery and hardware dealer in this part of the state. Mr. Thorbus was getting up in years, but his two sons, Clarence and Earl would someday take over the business. Earl was just a little younger than Logan, and they had been good friends for several years. But Clarence was who Logan intended to see. He had volunteered as a special deputy about the same time Logan became a regular deputy under Sheriff McMillan, and being a "friend of the family," they all knew Logan well.

"Well, hello Hans Logan!" Mr. Thorbus said when he saw the young deputy at the front door. He always had time to break away from whatever he was doing to greet Logan.

"Hello, Mr. Thorbus," Logan responded with a big grin. "How are you today?" He headed past the racks holding all sorts of shovels, axes, picks, and various tools to meet the old man. Half way there, his good friend Earl came bounding out from a doorway. "Hi, Logan!" he called out. "What brings you here?"

Logan shook hands with Mr. Thorbus and then handily put Earl to his knees in a brief, friendly arm wrestling match.

"Now, boys," Mr. Thorbus warned. "Better be careful with all these sharp objects close at hand."

"Actually," Logan said. "I need to talk to Clarence. Is he here today?" He released Earl and helped him back to his feet.

"I suspect he's out in the warehouse building," Mr. Thorbus said. "Earl... go with Logan and help him find Clarence. I have some customers to attend to."

"Okay, Pop," Earl replied. "C'mon, Logan. He's out back... this way." He headed out the door, motioning for Logan to follow. When they were crossing the yard to the warehouse he asked, "What d'ya need to talk to Clarence about?"

"It's official business... a message from Sheriff Colby."

"And ya can't tell me... right?"

"That's right. Sorry, Earl."

Looking a little crestfallen, Earl pointed to a door in the warehouse. "He's in there. I gotta go back up front."

"Earl," Logan said. "Sorry I can't tell you what this is about. It's kinda secret. You should tell the sheriff you want to be a special deputy. Then I could—"

"That's okay, Logan. Go take care of your business with Clarence. I'll see ya later."

"Clarence?" Logan called. His voice echoed in the long

building filled with plows and harrows and all sorts of farm implements.

"Logan!" came a reply from across the room, and then he saw Clarence hurrying toward him. "How have you been? I haven't seen you in a while."

"I've been fine, Clarence. And you?"

"Oh, I've been pretty occupied. Busy time of the year, y' know."

"Sure... well... the sheriff could use some extra hands tomorrow night, and he was wondering if you could come over to his office this afternoon for a meeting."

"I reckon I could get away for a little while. What time?"

"About one o'clock would be good."

"Okay, Logan. I'll be there."

"Thanks, Clarence. See ya then. Hafta run and find some of the others."

On his way to find Felix Henderson at the Cargill Grain Elevator, Logan thought about Sheriff Colby's reaction to all this. Something didn't seem right, and he started feeling uneasy about how the sheriff would handle the situation. This sheriff had no experience with such matters as train robbery. Of course, no one in the entire state had any such experience. The outlaws who engaged in these bold acts had stayed in the far western territories where there were fewer lawmen to hinder their choice of occupation, and where there were more unpopulated expanses in which to hide. Until now.

But it wasn't the lack of experience that Logan feared would turn this thing to possible disaster. Sheriff Colby had not promised to protect Jackson Evans, a fair exchange for exposing the gang's intensions to execute a serious crime.

Felix was easy to find—he was right outside the elevator office inspecting a wagonload of corn.

"Hey, Felix," Logan said as he rode Argo next to the wagon. "Real busy today?"

"Not really. Why?"

"Sheriff Colby would like you to come to his office for a meeting this afternoon... about one o'clock. Think you can make it?"

"I'll talk to Mr. Cargill, but I'm sure I can be there."

And so it went with four other special deputies at various places around town. If they all could be available Friday night, that would make a force of ten.

Raindrops that seemed as big as tree frogs started plummeting just as Logan approached City Livery. He darted inside on Argo's back without waiting for Mr. Benjamin. A cloudburst and gusty wind soon sent Mr. Benjamin and Logan scurrying to pull the big doors shut.

"Can I leave Argo here this afternoon," Logan said. "I'll be at the Sheriff's Office."

"Sure," Mr. Benjamin replied. "I'll take good care of him."

By the time the meeting was to start, the rain had diminished to mere sprinkles; all the deputies came streaming into the Sheriff's Office. Several extra wooden chairs had been placed in the room so everyone had a place to sit down.

"Afternoon, gentlemen," the sheriff greeted them as they came in. All the men were smiling and cheerful; they new nothing about the reason for the meeting. After a few minutes of chatter among them, the sheriff called for their attention.

"Logan has told me that he did not inform any of you why you were to come here today. So, we'll get right to it. I need your help tomorrow night to catch a band of train robbers."

Expressions all around the room turned solemn.

"Now, I know we ain't never had any opportunity to do this before," Colby explained. "But if we use our heads, I think we can get the upper hand on these guys."

A few mumbles erupted. "Who are we s'posed to be catching?" Felix asked. "The James Gang?"

"No," Colby replied. "But it seems we have a lost member from another gang... the Collins Gang."

George, Sam, and Logan already knew all this information, so they just calmly observed the special deputies exchanging confused, curious glances with each other.

"Weren't they all caught out in Kansas a few years back?" Clarence asked.

"It was Nebraska," Colby said. "And all but one... an outlaw by the name of Tom Nixon."

"How do you know he's gonna rob a train?"

"I got it from an informant... someone in the gang."

Logan rolled his eyes back.

Colby went on. "I sent a telegram to the sheriff in Deadwood where Nixon was hangin' his hat for a few years. He wired me back and confirmed that Nixon had never been caught..." Colby continued to explain how Charlie McCoy had been identified as Tom Nixon, and how he recruited a few local roughnecks to organize his gang, never once mentioning that Logan had actually gathered the information.

Colby continued. "They're gonna hit the Milwaukee and St. Paul tomorrow night when it pulls into the Rockland Depot at ten-fifteen."

"But Rockland isn't in this county," Clarence said.

"Well, two of the outlaws are getting on the train here in Sparta," Colby explained. "So that means we will be in legal pursuit."

"Pursuit?" Clarence said. "Aren't we gonna be hiding out, waiting for them at the depot?"

"No," Colby replied. "I've got a better idea. We'll be in the express car waiting for them."

More curious glances bounced around the room.

"We'll all leave town separately, at different times, and ride over to Tunnel City. We'll get on the train there."

When Colby finished explaining his scheme to combat the robbery plans, he laid out a schedule for all the deputies to leave town at various times so no one would be suspicious seeing the entire lot of them riding out together. Then he instructed them to be prepared for the worst—that there could be a gun battle, however, he was hopeful that could be avoided. But they had to be ready for anything, and they all had to be armed and carrying ample ammunition.

Colby dismissed his deputies from the meeting, confident that they were strong enough in number to handle the likes of an inexperienced gang of seven, whose leader was the only seasoned outlaw.

As soon as all the special deputies had left, Logan approached Sheriff Colby. "Will you need me for anything here this afternoon?"

Colby leaned back in his chair and glanced toward George and Sam. Then after a long pause he said, "No, I think we can handle things here."

"That's good... well then..." Logan said, a little nervousness showing in his voice. "I... I'd like to get Argo home in his barn before it starts raining again."

That didn't seem an unusual request; everyone knew how Logan loved and pampered that horse.

"Sure," Colby said. "You go on home... and it really won't be necessary for you to come back until tomorrow afternoon."

Chapter 24

O n the ride back to his father's farm, Logan had plenty of time to think about the developing events. He was fighting the urge to dismiss his instincts, because his instincts had always served him well. And now his instincts told him that something didn't seem right. The sheriff was acting peculiar, and at the meeting he hadn't wanted to suggest to the sheriff some possible alterations in the plan that could have offered safety to all those concerned. It seemed strange that Colby hadn't provided protection for the station agent who would be attacked before the train arrived. And Logan was still concerned about Jackson's safety. Colby seemed too eager to make use of the available firepower, and he had not offered any instructions to the men about not harming Jackson.

Something else about the sheriff's behavior bothered Logan; Colby was trying to hide the facts revealing the true source of his information about the robbery. Logan didn't really care that Colby wasn't giving him much credit, but Colby wasn't willing to give Jackson any recognition, either.

And Jackson would certainly be the center attraction when it came down to reporters and newspapers. Colby wanted all that for himself, and maybe that was the reason he wasn't concerned with Jackson's protection from the possible gunfire.

Logan knew it was probably risky to try to make contact with Jackson, mostly because of the temperament of the other gang members. His life could be in jeopardy if they saw him fraternizing with the law. But he had to warn Jackson, somehow.

Instead of riding directly to the farm, Logan went right into town. He needed a messenger to deliver a note to the boarding house. On Leonard Street he spotted a young boy tormenting a toad along the railroad tracks. He looked starved for candy.

"Hey," Logan said as he rode near. "You know where Mrs. Jorgenson's boarding house is?"

Reluctantly the boy replied, "Sure."

"I'll give you a nickel if you deliver a message there for me."

Visions of cinnamon sticks and gum drops glowed in the boy's eyes and he quickly abandoned the toad. "What's the message?" he asked.

Logan dug a piece of paper and a pencil out of his shirt pocket. He wrote simply: *Stones on the window tonight— important.*

Then he folded the paper a couple of times, wrote *Jackson* on the outside, and handed it to the boy.

"Where's my nickel?"

Logan retrieved some coins from his pants pocket, found a nickel and gave it to the boy. "Now, you give that note to

Mrs. Jorgenson... right away... before you go buyin' candy at the store. I'll be watchin' you."

The youngster seemed to understand the urgency in Logan's voice. "Okay, mister," he said, and started running up the street. Logan followed him to Franklin Street and watched him until he turned into the opening in the cedar hedge. He trusted Mrs. Jorgenson would get the note to Jackson, and he was quite certain that Jackson would understand the words that no one else would, should the note fall into the wrong hands.

Chapter 25

Jackson had put in a long day helping Mr. Abernathy with the new corrals. Building fences was as strenuous as cutting timber, but he knew now that he greatly preferred the warmer weather and sweating over wading through waist-deep snow and the numbing cold winter, despite the little rain shower that had soaked him earlier. He had grown to like Edwin Abernathy, though, and he hoped that Ed wouldn't shun him once word got out that he'd been involved with McCoy's gang. *But,* Jackson thought as he walked back to the boarding house, *if Mr. Abernathy fires me, I'll understand.*

And then he got to daydreaming about what his life might have become had he decided to stay loyal to Charlie McCoy—or Tom Nixon, the outlaw. He could have not said anything to Logan, helped the gang to be successful with the robbery, and in a couple of days he could ride away to parts unknown with ten thousand dollars in his saddlebag. He'd be rich!

But that would have come at a higher price than he was willing to pay. He would have betrayed his best friend, Logan. He would have disgraced his family, and he probably would never see them again. And he would be a wanted man, on the run for the rest of his life, just like Tom Nixon, living a life of lies and deception, assuming false names and always having to cover his tracks. That is… if he didn't get caught during the robbery and thrown in jail, or worse yet, get shot and killed. He didn't much care for any of those options.

There was no doubt in his mind that he had chosen the right thing to do. He couldn't run away from the gang; he knew that. But he felt obligated to Logan, and following Logan's coaching to appear loyal to the gang right up until the robbery was the best help he could give.

Millie Jorgenson met him at the door. "Hello, Jackson," she said and beamed a cheerful smile. "A little boy came by dis afternoon. He left you dis note."

"Who? What little boy?"

"I think he might be one of the Anderson children, but I can't be sure."

"But I don't know the Anderson children. Why would he be leaving me a note?" Puzzled, Jackson unfolded the paper.

"I don't know," said Millie. "He yust said he vas supposed to bring me dis note, but it has your name on it, and I have no idea what it means."

Jackson silently read: *Stones on the window tonight— important.*

There was no signature, but it only took a few seconds for Jackson to determine who the note had come from, and what it meant. "It's okay, Mrs. Jorgenson." He frowned and refolded the paper. "I know what it is. Don't you worry about a thing." Then he ran up the stairs to his room, closed and locked the door, and sat on the edge of his bed. He carefully unfolded the paper once more and read the message again. Clearly, this was Logan's way of telling him something had possibly gone wrong. *Why does he need to talk to me tonight?* he pondered.

The supper bell rang precisely at six o'clock. Jackson hid the note under his pillow and calmly walked down to the dining room. Charlie hadn't eaten supper at the boarding house since the final plans for the train robbery had been made and he had received his last pay from Edwin Abernathy. Jackson didn't know where McCoy was eating his supper now, but he didn't care. He was glad it wasn't here.

He sat down at the table across from Henry Good and Victor Johnson, just as he had always done. They noticed right away that something seemed to be bothering him. "Not feeling well?" Victor asked.

"Oh, I'm feeling fine," Jackson responded. "Just a little tired, I guess."

"Millie!" Victor said. She was standing next to Jackson with a large platter of fried trout that she said Jacob had caught that morning. "Millie! You ain't feedin' the boy enough. That must be why he's tired."

Millicent looked down at Jackson. "Vell, den," she said in that wonderful Scandinavian accent. "Jackson? You help yourself to an extra piece of fish." She winked at the boy. "You might as vell take Mr. Johnson's share, too."

Jackson patted Millie's arm. "That's okay, Millie. You're feedin' me just fine. And I wouldn't want Mr. Johnson to go hungry tonight."

They all laughed and dug into the delicious supper. A few minutes later, Henry Good asked, "Where's your friend, Charlie? Haven't seen him here for supper for a while."

Jackson could feel his face turn a warm shade of red. "Don't know. I... I haven't seen him since he quit workin' for Mr. Abernathy."

"Sure was a curious sort of fellow," Henry said. "Where'd he say he come from?"

"Michigan," said Jackson. Then, with hopes of changing the subject he said, "Hey, Jacob. Where did you catch these trout?"

Jacob looked up from his plate at the far end of the table. "Well, if I told ye that, you'd tell ever' other dang fool from Sparta t' La Crosse, an' they'd go ketch 'em all, an' then there wouldn't be none left for us." He went back to eating his supper.

Jackson lay in his bed that night, anxiously waiting for the house to be totally quiet so he knew everyone had drifted off to sleep. It was nearly midnight when he only heard sounds of snoring. He waited a while, just to be sure, and then snuck down the stairs with boots in hand. A cloudy, stormy sky had remained since that morning, making well bottom darkness, and crossing the river below the dam rather difficult. He gathered a few stones and stumbled on through the black night to Logan's place.

A faint light shone in Logan's window. He had thoughtfully left a lamp burning to help Jackson find his way on such a dark night.

Plink.

Only one stone was necessary on this night. Logan instantly appeared at the window. "I'll be right down," he called out in a loud whisper. He didn't have to see Jackson to know he was there.

He came out the front door hoisting a lantern shoulder-high, illuminating the yard. Jackson stood still, waiting for his friend to come near, and then they walked together quickly to the barn. Argo and Apollo nickered softly when they entered and Logan hung the lantern from a hook on a rafter.

"So... what's so important?" Jackson asked.

Logan leaned against Argo's stall. He stared at Jackson, and Jackson could see the worry in his eyes. "You might be in danger," Logan finally said.

Jackson returned the stare with a satirical laugh. "I'm keeping company with a band of blood-thirsty outlaws! Yeah! I know I'm in danger!"

"No..." Logan said. "I mean with the sheriff and his deputies."

"What d'ya mean?"

Logan stepped close and put his hand on Jackson's shoulder. "The sheriff and all his deputies, including me, will be on that train tomorrow night."

"Huh?"

"We're all riding over to Tunnel City and boarding there. When it stops in Rockland, there's apt to be some shooting, and I don't think the sheriff has any intentions of making sure *you* don't get shot."

Jackson's face turned pale. "But why? I'm helping him get Tom Nixon."

"I know that," Logan said. "But I've got it all figured out. Colby wants to take all the credit for capturing a wanted outlaw, and he's afraid you'll draw a lot of attention after the dust settles as being the one who really discovered Nixon."

"So... what am I s'posed to do?"

"We have to figure out a way for you not to be there when that train arrives at Rockland... without the others getting suspicious."

"I'll be guarding the station agent... alone. Maybe I could just slip out when everybody else is busy robbing the train."

"No... too risky. If one of the deputies sees you runnin' off, you'll get yourself shot."

"Well... have you got any better idea?"

Logan sat down on the hay. "No," he said, sounding quite discouraged. "Unfortunately, I don't have a better idea."

"I'll be okay," Jackson assured. "It'll be dark. I'll find a place to hide... and you can find me later."

Chapter 26

Friday morning's sunrise didn't promise much brightness —only more clouds and gray dreariness, and the smell of rain lingered in the air. Logan would have preferred a little sunshine to rain, because he was quite sure that Argo might be out all day. But if the clouds stayed, the night would be darker, and that would certainly give Jackson the advantage if he had to flee into hiding.

For Jackson, it had to be just another day. He sensed that Charlie would be watching him, so he dared not do anything out of the ordinary. After breakfast he walked the mile out of town to Abernathy's farm, just as he usually did, and began his task of setting more posts for the new fence. All day he expected Charlie to appear, like some dark, sinister ogre sent by Satin.

The day they had planned for was here. Now it was down to a just few hours when Charlie McCoy would return to his former life of crime and violence as Tom Nixon. Jackson knew, however, that this day wouldn't end the way Charlie had intended it to end. He wouldn't be riding off into the darkness carrying $75,000 in his saddlebag. More than likely, he would be riding off to spend a good many years behind bars, where he belonged.

By the time Logan arrived in Sparta, only the sheriff remained—all the other deputies had left town to make their rendezvous at Tunnel City. Logan suspected that he and Colby might ride together and that he would have the opportunity to persuade the sheriff to make sure no harm came to Jackson. This would be, perhaps, his last chance to find out if Colby intended to prevent Jackson from ever revealing the fact that it was he who was responsible for averting the great train robbery. His speech was planned, practiced and polished. A few minutes of time alone with the sheriff might change the outcome of what could very easily turn into disaster.

"Ah, Logan," the sheriff smiled a greeting. "Glad you're here. I have a special assignment for you... very important."

Logan thought for an instant that perhaps Colby had decided to post a deputy at Rockland after all, and that he was the chosen one. That would certainly simplify his efforts to protect Jackson.

The sheriff reached to his desk and grasped a large, sealed thick envelope. He held it toward Logan. "You have just enough time to catch the afternoon westbound train." He peered at the big clock on the wall. "It leaves at three-forty-five. These papers have to be delivered to the county clerk's office at the courthouse in La Crosse today."

"But Sheriff," Logan protested. "What about—"

"No time to chat now. You only have a few minutes to get to the depot."

"But what about Argo? I can't just leave him here."

"I'll ride with you to the depot and I'll take Argo back to the livery for you. He'll be fine."

In a matter of moments, Colby had Logan to the door. "Here's money for your fare to and from La Crosse." He handed Logan three silver dollars. "And a little extra for your supper, too."

"But what about tonight?" Logan asked as the sheriff whisked him down the steps to where the horses were tied.

"Don't you worry 'bout tonight. I've got plenty of men to cover that."

They were riding at a fast pace down Water Street toward the railroad depot when Logan asked, "But Sheriff... I should be there, too. I'm the best man with a gun that you have."

"I know that, Logan. And so do the outlaws. Everybody for miles around knows you're the best shot anywhere around here. You're the first one they'd aim at. I don't want you gettin' shot."

That explanation coming from the sheriff took Logan by surprise. It sounded sincere, and for a moment Logan thought maybe he had misjudged Colby. But he wasn't thoroughly convinced. "Is that the only reason you chose me to go to La Crosse?"

"No! Those papers really have to be delivered today."

"You could've sent one of the special deputies."

"They've already left for Tunnel City."

"Jackson is helping you," Logan said in desperation. "You know that, don't you? Promise me he won't get hurt."

"I'll see what I can do."

The whistle blew just as they rode up to the depot. "You can catch a train back later tonight," Colby said. "I'll still need you to help with the prisoners."

Or help with hauling away corpses Logan thought as he jumped aboard the train only moments before it started rolling. He looked back through the window to see Colby riding away, leading Argo, and then found an empty seat where he waited for the conductor to come by to collect his fare. Visions of everything going wrong raced through his head, and he couldn't clear his mind of the thought that

Colby had purposely sent him away for all the wrong reasons. Jackson was in more danger than he realized, but now Logan feared that the entire situation was out of his reach, and there was nothing more he could do to help. He was so bogged down with all of this that the conductor had to tap him on the shoulder to get his attention. "How far y' goin' deputy?" the conductor asked, staring at Logan's badge.

"Oh! La Crosse," Logan answered.

"That'll be seventy-five cents."

Logan handed the conductor a silver dollar. As the conductor gave him his change, Logan asked, "How long does this train stop in West Salem?"

"Ten minutes. No more. No less."

Logan's quick thinking had produced one last effort to help Jackson. "I have to deliver a very important message to the station porter—Henry Good—when we pass through there. It's official police business. I'll need to get off the train to talk to him. Hold the train until I get back on." Logan knew Henry Good lived at the boarding house, and he knew he could trust him to get a message to Jackson.

The conductor eyed Logan's badge on the front of his vest. Reluctantly he agreed. "Okay, but don't take too long. We have a schedule, y' know."

"Thank you, sir. I'll make it as fast as I can."

The train made a whistle stop in Rockland—long enough for the express man and the station agent to exchange mail bags. Only one passenger boarded.

Logan studied the big rocks off to the left, and the station house on the right, and just beyond lay the little town of Rockland. He hoped and secretly prayed that this would not be the site of a bloody massacre later that night.

A few minutes later the train stopped briefly again at Bangor, and Logan knew in just ten minutes more they would arrive at West Salem. He would be waiting at the door and ready to disembark as soon as the train stopped.

When his feet hit the platform at West Salem, his eyes were already scanning the depot area for Henry Good. Several passengers were waiting to board the train, and Henry was there too, probably to render any needed assistance. Logan ran to him and grabbed his arm, pulling him aside.

"Logan!" Henry said, astonished. "What's the matter?"

Logan stared deeply into Henry's eyes. "Henry," he said quietly. "I need you to get a message to Jackson at the boarding house where you live. It's a matter of... life and death."

Henry saw the sincerity on Logan's face, and he recognized the urgency. "Okay. I'll see him at supper tonight."

"No. Don't wait for supper. Get to him as soon as you can. This can't wait."

"All right... I'll find him as soon as he comes back from the farm."

"Good. That will be fine. You tell him that the sheriff sent me to La Crosse on the train, and that I won't be at Rockland tonight. He'll know what you mean. And tell him that I'll be coming back on the later train and I'll look for him."

"But what—"

"I can't tell you any more, Henry. Just give him that message. He'll know what it all means."

"Okay," Henry said.

Logan saw that Henry was puzzled, but he knew he couldn't say any more, for Jackson's safety's sake. "Oh. And one more thing, Henry... don't let anyone else hear. Make absolutely sure that you and Jackson are alone. Okay?"

"Okay."

"Henry," Logan said as if pleading. "I must count on you."

Henry nodded and smiled. "You can count on me, Logan."

Chapter 27

"Y' know, Joshua?" Jacob said as he bellied up to the bar. "Funniest thing... I just came from Sparta, and y' know what?"

The barkeeper looked at the old hunter with indifference as he drew Jacob's usual beer. "No. What?"

"Thar ain't a lawman left in that whole town. They's all just up and left. Ain't a dern one there!"

Joshua abruptly stopped wiping the bar. His eyes narrowed to slits. "How do you know that, Jacob?"

"Well... I was out checkin' on my muskrat traps and doin' a little fishin' and I seen ever' one of 'em leave town."

"Where were they going?"

"Derned if I know. Didn't pay no attention to which way they headed. Just seen 'em leave... one by one."

"Well, thank you, Jacob. The beer's on me today."

It hadn't taken Joshua long to speculate why every lawman in Sparta had left town. Somehow, the gang's plan for the train heist had slipped out. Whether it had been coincidence or there was a traitor among them he didn't know, but now there wasn't time to investigate that matter. More importantly, now, he had to get word to all the gang and abort the holdup. Another opportunity would avail them some other time, some other place. But right now, there was too much risk in attempting to carry out their present plan.

He quickly found paper and pencil and wrote notes to each gang member:

Law knows our plan. Must cancel tonight. Don't go. Joshua.

He gave the notes to Wendell. He'd delivered messages to all the gang members before, so he knew where to find them. Joshua trusted the boy, and he didn't worry about him saying anything to anyone he shouldn't; Wendell wasn't smart enough to know his task was for a criminal. He just knew he'd earn a dollar for his efforts.

Wendell hustled off, first to the McMillan mill to find Max Jensen and Eddy Slokum. Then he ran to the boarding house on Franklin Street, and without knocking on the front door, he went inside, snuck up the stairs and down the hall to Jackson's door. He knocked, but there was no answer, so he slid the note under the door.

Wendell then dashed off to Louis Reed's Livery on Church Street, and then cut across to Leonard Street by way of the railroad tracks. He delivered the note to John Schultz at his rented room above the hardware store, and then finally to the hotel and Charlie McCoy's room.

Charlie heard the knock on his door. "Who's there?"

"Wendell," came the faint answer. "I got a note for you... from Joshua."

Charlie opened the door. Wendell stood there with the note held out at arm's length. Charlie took the note, quickly unfolded the paper and read the short message. Wendell turned to leave, but McCoy caught him by his shirt collar. "Hold on, there, boy," Charlie said. "Did Joshua tell you anything else?"

"No, sir," the boy replied.

Charlie pulled the boy into his room and closed the door. "You wait right here," he told Wendell. Wheels were turning and whistles were blowing and dynamite was exploding inside his head. He turned to the bureau, pulled open a drawer and retrieved several sheets of writing paper and a pencil. He wrote notes to each gang member:

We hit the EAST bound train tonight like we originally planned. Stop the train at Miller's Crossing 9:30. McCoy.

Charlie wasn't willing to give up so easily. This had been their first plan until they found out about the payroll money on the westbound train. Jesse James and his gang had been quite successful with train holdups out in the middle of nowhere, in the middle of the night, and there was no reason why this couldn't work for this gang, too. All the members knew the plan, and so any further explanation wasn't necessary. Charlie gave the folded notes to Wendell. "Now, take the notes to everybody," he barked. "You don't have to take one to Jackson at the boarding house. I'll see him myself."

"But Joshua pays me a dollar to bring his notes to you."

"Okay," Charlie said sharply. He dug in his pocket. "Here's a dollar."

The boy took the notes and ran off, first to the mill, where he learned that Max and Eddy had left. Mr. McMillan said they had gone hunting for a couple of days.

Wendell attempted to deliver the rest of the notes with no success; Louis Reed had closed the livery for the night; John Schultz was no longer in his room; Joshua had left the saloon in his hired bartender's hands.

Jackson had just returned to his room from a long day at the farm. And while Wendell attempted to deliver the rest of the notes, Jackson picked the paper from the floor, but before he opened and read the note, he heard a knock on his door.

His heart pounded. He was certain it was Charlie in the hall.

"Who is it?" he said.

"Henry," a familiar voice answered softly. "I have a message for you from Deputy Logan. He said it's important."

Jackson threw open the door, sighing in relief that it wasn't Charlie. He stared at Henry Good standing in his doorway.

"Can I come in?" Henry said. "No one else is s'posed to hear this." He nervously looked down the hall to make sure no one else was there.

"Yes, come in," Jackson said, and immediately closed the door when Henry was inside.

"Logan said you'd know what this was about..."

"Okay. What did he say?"

"He told me to tell you that the sheriff sent him to La Crosse, and that he wouldn't be in Rockland tonight. He's coming back on a late train, and he'll look for you then."

The words shocked Jackson. His eyes glazed in a moment of fear, and he stood there, as if he were unable to speak another word.

"Are you all right?" Henry asked. He grasped Jackson's arms just below the shoulder. "Is there any way I can help?"

Jackson snapped out of his visions of how he imagined a blaze of gunfire would appear in the night. He shook his head and backed away from Henry. "I'm okay, Henry. Really." He looked down at the paper in his hand, and then opened the door for Henry to leave.

Henry could read the distress in Jackson's face and he wondered if he should try to offer more assistance.

"I'm okay, Henry," Jackson repeated. "I'll see you later at supper."

Henry stepped out into the hallway and Jackson closed the door. Then he looked down at the paper again, unfolded it and read the short note from Joshua. Another sigh of relief escaped from his tightened chest as the words on the paper poked through his anxiety and settled the jitters he'd been feeling in his gut all day.

He stripped off his dirty work clothes and fell back on his bed, relaxed. He thought about Logan and how he and the sheriff and all the deputies would find nothing at Rockland but a peaceful little town with nothing out of the ordinary happening when the train arrived at 10:15. No robbers. No guns. No dynamite. Just an ordinary mail stop in the middle of the night.

The supper bell clanged, and Jackson came to from a trance that had almost put him to sleep. He jumped out of bed, hastily washed his hands and face, slipped on a clean shirt, trousers and boots, combed his hair and hurried down to the dining room.

After supper, Jackson joined Henry Good and Victor Johnson out on the front porch. He listened to them talking about the excellent meal they had just eaten—how juicy the fried chicken was and how last year's canned vegetables from Millie's garden still tasted pretty good. And then they talked about the weather, and how any more rain might raise the river. There had been a heavy cloud cover all day, and now their darkness was quickly swallowing the daylight.

Jackson thought he owed Henry an explanation for the mysterious message he had delivered that afternoon, and he was waiting for an opportunity to talk to Henry alone. But he never got the chance.

About 8:30 Jackson saw a man just beyond the cedar

hedge, and in the grayness of dusk he recognized the familiar figure—Charlie McCoy.

"Hey, Jackson," Charlie called out, before Jackson had a chance to slip out of sight. "Git yer hat and come on out here. We're goin' for a little walk."

Jackson felt his chest tighten up again. He thought he was finally rid of Charlie McCoy, but apparently he was not. He slowly rose from his chair and went to his room for his hat. While he was there, he saw the note from Joshua; he slipped it into his pocket.

Out at the cedar hedge, Charlie waited impatiently.

"Where are we going?" Jackson asked quietly.

"Let's go." Charlie said.

Jackson followed Charlie into the darkness. At first, he thought that maybe this was Charlie's way of saying good-bye, that he wanted some privacy out in the country to say it. But Charlie was acting rather strangely. This wasn't a good-bye party. Charlie had something brewing.

Chapter 28

L ogan walked the distance back to the railroad depot on the north side of La Crosse. He had plenty of time to catch the next train. When he entered the station, he located a chart on the wall that showed time schedules of arrivals and departures at all the stops from La Crosse to Milwaukee. The next eastbound train leaving La Crosse would arrive in Sparta at 9:45; the westbound train that the sheriff and deputies were riding would pull into Sparta ten minutes later, at 9:55. If both trains were on schedule, Logan thought he might have a chance to board the westbound. But he knew that two of the gang were to board that train at Sparta so he'd have to do it without being seen. He had an idea.

The train would be stopped in La Crosse for a full half-hour to take on coal and water. He'd have enough time to investigate his idea, and if he couldn't get the cooperation he needed, he'd still be able to board the passenger car in time.

The eastbound 8:05 arrived right on time, huffing and belching billows of black smoke and clouds of white steam that hung in the warm, humid air. Twenty or thirty people scurried toward the passenger cars while two porters in their black uniforms and caps pushed carts piled high with suitcases and steamer trunks toward the baggage car.

Logan casually walked to the locomotive as the smoke and steam slowly cleared. He considered his options as to how he would get the cooperation he needed. He could be meek and polite and ask the engineer for permission to ride on the tender to Sparta; or he could exercise his authority and *tell* the engineer he was riding the tender to Sparta. A voice inside his head told him the latter was the wiser choice.

The engineer was applying thick, tar-like oil from a spouted can to various parts on the side of the massive black machinery. Logan felt the heat radiate from the boiler; he heard the sizzle and hiss of steam; the smell of hot oil and iron wafted to his nostrils.

"Excuse me, sir," he said as the engineer turned, noticing Logan approaching.

He was tall and wiry looking, and his bib overalls had once been blue but now were mostly black from oil, coal dust and soot. The high-crowned cap on his head was nearly as black, and his bulky leather gloves were blacker. "What can I do fer ya?" he said in a gruff tone.

"I'm Deputy Sheriff Hans Logan. I will be riding in the tender car to Sparta."

The engineer studied Logan for a long moment, eyed the shiny badge on his vest and the holstered six-shooter at his hip. "What the hell ya wanna do that fer?"

"I need to get off this train in Sparta without being seen, and I figure I can do that from here."

"Is there some kinda trouble?"

"Could be."

"Well... suit yerself. Ain't the cleanest place to ride, y' know."

Chapter 29

J ackson soon understood this meeting was not meant as a farewell party. Charlie seemed far to tense as they walked toward the edge of town. They heard the not-so-distant whistle from the approaching eastbound.

Charlie stopped and turned toward Jackson. "We don't have time to make it to Bangor. We'll get on the train here."

"What are you talking about?" Jackson asked.

"Remember our first plan? To hit the eastbound at Miller's Crossing?"

"Yeah."

"Well, that's what we're gonna do." He leaned into some bushes along the tracks and pulled out a double-barrel shotgun, a lever action Winchester rifle, and a box of ammunition that he had stashed there earlier.

"But Joshua canceled—"

"I sent messages to everybody. They'll be waiting in the woods at Miller's Crossing. Just like we planned. And they'll have two extra horses for us." He handed the shotgun to Jackson and then dug out four shells from the box. "The gun is loaded. Put these extra shells in your pocket."

Jackson stood there, numb with bewilderment as he accepted the weapon and ammo. He didn't know what to say, but he realized that he had to follow Charlie's lead or his body would be found at daylight in the ditch next to the tracks.

They made their way into the dark shadows of the trees and buildings on the south side of the tracks, opposite the depot, just before the eastbound rumbled to a stop, spewing its usual curtain of black smoke and steam. Charlie nudged Jackson and pointed to the baggage car just ahead of the first passenger coach. "When the train starts moving," he said, "You jump onto the back of that car. Climb the ladder up to the roof and then lay low up there until we're through Bangor and Rockland. I'll be on the roof of the express car right ahead of you."

Jackson nodded to acknowledge Charlie's instructions. They had worked out this plan long ago, and he knew that Charlie intended to surprise the engineer and fireman from behind after the train pulled out of Rockland and would force them at gunpoint to stop the train as it approached Miller's Crossing where the rest of the gang waited in the woods to complete the attack. It was a good plan, and especially on this night that was so dark because of the cloudy sky. They would make their getaway into the hills and would be seen by no one.

But Jackson didn't want any part of it. He momentarily recalled the relief he had felt just a few hours earlier when he read the note from Joshua, and he knew he could not—would not—participate in this criminal act. Yes, the odds of getting away were quite favorable; the sheriff and all his deputies would be aboard the westbound train, focused on Rockland, while the actual robbery had already occurred a half-hour before on the eastbound train.

Time had run out for Jackson, and now there was no chance to warn the sheriff of the changed plans. He would just have to play along with Charlie until he saw an opportunity for a safe escape.

The train had been at a standstill at the West Salem depot for exactly ten minutes when a couple of short whistle blasts sounded.

"Okay," Charlie said. "Get ready to run for the baggage car."

Jackson nodded, gripped the shotgun tightly, and waited for the train to start rolling, and for Charlie to make the first move.

Another sharp blast from the locomotive's whistle pierced the darkness, and then puffs of exhausting steam from the engine pounded the dense, humid air like a bass drum in a Fourth of July parade. Jackson could feel the pounding, but he was sure it was his own heart thumping.

"Okay! Go!" Charlie said. He gave Jackson a push toward the moving train. The boy had no choice but to keep up the pace as Charlie maintained a firm grip on his shirt sleeve. In mere seconds they were within gripping distance of the small platform at the rear of the baggage car. Charlie gave him a boost to help him get onto the platform.

Jackson grasped the ladder rung and watched as Charlie ran alongside the train that was gradually gaining speed. Charlie reached for the platform railing at the rear of the express car, swung himself aboard, and quickly started climbing toward the roof.

Jackson thought this might be the opportunity he needed. In a split-second he made his decision. Charlie was occupied with climbing and he would not see, and the noise of the engine and the wheels on the track would mask the sound of his boots hitting the ground. Jackson released his grip on the ladder and hurtled his weight clear of the moving train without even a thought about waiting to choose a soft landing spot.

Anything short of a feather bed would not be soft when

leaping from a train moving at 15 miles per hour. Jackson's feet hit the hard ground amidst a patch of weeds. His knees buckled under him. He tumbled and rolled, and when he came to rest he lay still for a few moments wondering if he were still alive. He no longer held the shotgun; he could remember dropping it when he fell, but he didn't care where it was now. The last car of the train passed him, and then it faded out of sight into the darkness among the trees that lined both sides of the tracks. Charlie was on his way to rob a train, but he would be doing it without his sidekick.

This had happened all too quickly, and now, Jackson had to evaluate the state of affairs, sort it all out to make some sense, and determine what to do, if anything. *The sheriff and his posse are thirty miles away at Tunnel City. Logan is in La Crosse waiting for a later train. WAIT A MINUTE! This was the later train. Logan is on that train with Charlie!*

Jackson bolted upright, nearly in panic. He thought he should do *something*, but he didn't know what.

Calm down, he told himself, and tried to think logically. *Maybe the train hasn't left Tunnel City yet. Maybe a telegram can reach the sheriff in time.* He turned and started running back to the railroad depot. The door had been propped open to let in a little air. Completely void of any other people by that time, Jackson had no trouble getting to the window where the station agent would be—he was the telegrapher, too.

"You hafta send a telegram to the sheriff," Jackson said. His voice was high-pitched and panic-stricken. "He's at the depot waiting for the westbound train in Tunnel City."

The agent was certainly taken aback by the boy's excitement. He saw cuts and bruises on Jackson's face and the tattered shirt that had taken quite a beating in the rough landing along the railroad tracks. His hat was gone and his hair mussed. Even Jackson didn't realize his appearance. The agent seemed to recognize the urgency and dismissed the possibility of this being a prank. "What's wrong, boy?" the agent said. "Has there been an accident?"

"No," Jackson said, excitement still in his words. "Just listen... please... let me explain. Then send a telegram to the sheriff before the train leaves Tunnel City." He paused to take notice of the agent's expression. It appeared that he acknowledged Jackson's plea with a nod. Jackson took a deep breath and began. "There's gonna be a robbery on the eastbound train at Miller's Crossing, but the sheriff thinks it's gonna be on the westbound at Rockland. That's why he and his men are gonna be on that train. But the plans got changed and now the gang is hitting the eastbound train instead. Charlie McCoy is on the eastbound now, and he thinks I'm there too, but I jumped off the train when he wasn't looking. The sheriff will know my name—it's Jackson Evans—I'm the reason he knew about the westbound robbery."

When Jackson quite talking, the agent looked up from scribbling some notes on a pad of paper. "Is that it?" he asked.

Jackson nodded. "That's enough," he said. "The sheriff will understand. Now, I don't have much time. I gotta go." And with that said he was out the door on a dead run. He hoped the agent would get the telegram sent in time. Right now, though, he needed to get a horse. All the horses would be gone from Reed's livery stable, and there was only one other place Jackson knew where he could get one—the

Logan farm. Apollo would be in the barn. Apollo knew him and wouldn't be spooked by a stranger. And Apollo was fast.

When Jackson reached the river, he had to stop for a few seconds to catch his breath, but he knew he couldn't take too long. It didn't occur to him that he could not possibly get to Miller's crossing ahead of the train—even on Apollo—but his concern for Logan's safety was overbearing, and nothing else really mattered.

Chapter 30

"**N**ow, men," Sheriff Colby said. He and the deputies were huddled in a tight group outside the Tunnel City depot waiting for the conductor to tell them to board the express car. "After the train pulls out of Sparta," he went on in almost a whisper, "We have to be ready." He pointed to one of the special deputies. "I want you in the first passenger coach. You'll get off as quickly as possible at the Rockland depot and go inside. There will be a kid guarding the station agent. Make sure that kid doesn't walk away... got it?"

The deputy nodded. "Yes, sir."

"The rest of us will be in the express car waiting for Nixon and Schultz to—"

"Sheriff Colby!" a frantic voice called out from the depot doorway. "Sheriff Colby... there's a telegram for you. It's urgent." The telegrapher handed Colby the message.

To Sheriff Colby:

Gang plans have changed. Gang waiting at Miller's Crossing to stop and rob eastbound train tonight. Charlie McCoy aboard that train now. Thinks I am aboard with him, but I am not.

Jackson Evans.

"Dammit!" Colby screamed when he had read the telegram. Then he turned to the conductor standing next to the passenger coach. "Conductor," he barked. "Things have changed. We'll all be getting on the passenger car. And tell the engineer to get this train rolling as fast as it will go toward Sparta.   Tell him *not to stop* until he sees that eastbound train. We don't have a minute to waste."

Sheriff Colby herded all his men onto the coach.   Then he made several people move to different seats so the posse could occupy the entire end of the car.   The deputies all faced him as he took a stand in the aisle between them.

"They must have found out somehow that we knew their plans," the sheriff said.   "They've changed their plan to stop the eastbound train at Miller's Crossing."

"Miller's Crossing!" George Clark said.   "Why, that's in our county!"

"That's right, it is," the sheriff said.   "Let's just hope this pile of iron can get us there in time."

"And if it doesn't?" Clarence Thorbus said.

Colby sat down on a vacant seat, took off his hat, and wiped his hand across his much stressed expression.   He looked straight ahead as if searching the distance for an answer.   "I guess then we'll have to head out in full force on a man hunt."

"They'll have quite a head start on us. I'd bet they have horses there with them."

"Sure they have horses. We'll have to pick up their trail at daylight."

"Well, Sheriff," George Clark said.   "We already know where they're going. Didn't Logan say they were gonna meet at Hillsboro to split up the loot?"

Chapter 31

J ackson was fully aware that he had strayed from the good and honest character he had been raised with, and now the evil side of him was haunting his soul. He didn't know what he could do, now, to help Logan, but he felt that he had to try to redeem himself, and in the process, perhaps some stroke of luck would help Logan, too. As he stepped carefully across the rocks below the dam, it occurred to him that he was about to steal Logan's horse, Apollo. Not that he was really stealing it, but that's how it would appear. Regardless of all that he had done so far, he was not a horse thief—or *any* kind of thief.

Thankful that he had made this journey to Logan's farm several times in the dark, he headed straight for the front door of the house and pounded with his fist, making as much noise as he could. "Mr. Logan!" he called out loudly. "Mr. Logan! Wake up! It's me... Jackson Evans!" He continued pounding on the door until he noticed a faint light through the window. It seemed to be moving closer, and finally the door swung open. Mr. Logan held a small oil lantern giving off just enough light for Jackson to see the man dressed only in a long night shirt. He didn't take the time to apologize for the late night intrusion.

"Mr. Logan... I need to take Apollo. Logan... er... your son, that is... could be in trouble, and I need to help him. I didn't want you to think I was stealing Apollo."

"Well, Jackson," said Mr. Logan. "What kind of trouble? Where?"

"There's gonna be a train holdup over at Miller's

Crossing, only Logan doesn't know it's gonna happen on the train he's on right now coming back from La Crosse."

It took a few seconds for all this to make sense to Mr. Logan. His eyes widened as he came to understand what Jackson was saying. "Okay, Jackson. You go ahead and take Apollo. I'll get dressed and come too. But don't wait for me. I'll be along in a little while."

"Thanks, Mr. Logan." Jackson turned to head for the barn at a run. He heard Mr. Logan call out to him, "And be careful, son!"

When Jackson entered the barn and lit the lantern Apollo nickered and bobbed his head as if greeting an old friend. He talked to the horse as if a person all the while he quickly put on the saddle and bridle, and when Jackson mounted, Apollo seemed to understand the importance of their mission. He galloped past Mr. Logan, just then on his way to the barn to saddle another horse.

Jackson was amazed at how Apollo's animal instinct guided them so accurately, so rapidly, through such a dark night. He splashed across the river and then carried Jackson gallantly through town to the east road.

Apollo galloped through the darkness along the wagon road that coursed through the valley, paralleling the railroad tracks, sometimes closely, and sometimes not. But Jackson was quite sure he would see the train even at a distance because there would be lights showing from the passenger car windows. He had worried some at first about the treacherous darkness, but now he was feeling confident in Apollo's sure-footed dash through the night.

He tried to imagine what would happen at Miller's Crossing. If everything went as they had first planned,

Charlie would jump down onto the coal tender, and then at gunpoint he would force the engineer to stop the train. The others would be waiting in the woods, all spread out, and they'd come out shooting in the air, making it sound as if a whole army was there, to intimidate the crew and passengers. Then Schultz and Joshua would get into the express car. Schultz would do his magic to the safe with a stick of dynamite while Joshua kept the express agent out of the way. Once the safe was emptied, they'd get off the train and disappear into the woods again where the horses were tied, well out of sight. By the time the train got rolling again and reached Sparta, the bandits would be long gone into the hills.

Jackson knew that if Logan was on that train, he would not sit still while all this was going on. He would not be intimidated by the gunfire; he would quickly calculate a means to attempt to stop the robbery somehow, perhaps exiting the coach on the back side and sneaking up on the robbers. Jackson had come to learn that Charlie and Joshua were callus to bloodshed, and as ruthless as they were, they would not hesitate to shoot to kill. Alone, Logan didn't stand a chance.

Chapter 32

Charlie lay flat on the roof of the express car, clutching the rifle with one hand and his hat with the other, not moving a muscle. He had been unnoticed during the five-minute stop at Bangor, and he was confident that the darkness was keeping him well concealed here, too, at Rockland. He couldn't even see back to the roof of the next car where Jackson should be.

Rockland was usually just a whistle stop at this time of night—long enough to toss off a mail bag, providing there were no passengers to board or disembark. And tonight, there were no passengers. The train started moving again almost immediately after stopping, and Charlie knew he had to get ready to move soon. Miller's Crossing was only about two miles. He pressed his hat down tightly on his head and rose up on one elbow. Smoke and soot from the engine blew into his face; he tipped his head so his hat brim protected his eyes while he pulled the bright red silk bandana up over his nose. Then he crawled to the front of the car. From there he could see the engineer and the fireman in the light of the engine's firebox.

He got to his knees and then stood, crouching for a few seconds, calculating the jump he would have to make down onto the coal in the tender that he could just barely see. This was the moment he had been anticipating. Without further hesitation he leapt forward. The noise from the engine covered any noise his boots made as he dropped onto the coal.

Miller's Crossing was just beyond a heavily wooded area

that the tracks passed through, and Charlie could tell they were passing through the woods now. He stood up on top of the coal and leveled the rifle toward the back of the engine.

"Throw up your hands!" Charlie yelled.

The engineer and fireman clearly heard the command. They turned toward the voice. The orange glow from the firebox cast its light on the masked bandit, and they definitely saw the rifle aimed at them. The two instantly complied with the order and raised their arms above their heads. It was now Charlie's intension to get closer, and to instruct them to slow the train to a stop at the edge of the woods.

But in the darkness, he failed to see Logan sitting on the coal in the shadows of the front corner of the tender. Logan heard him yell his order to the engineer. Charlie just barely noticed his movement when he turned. In the couple of seconds that it took for Logan to process the thought of what was happening and to grab for his revolver, Charlie had pointed the rifle in the general direction of the movement he had seen and fired a shot. Logan saw the muzzle flash. Instantly a sharp pain stung his left shoulder. He realized that the bullet had ripped into him, and he fell back into the corner. As he heard the lever action of the rifle deliver another round into the chamber, he raised his revolver and squeezed off a shot, but it missed its mark. Another deafening shot blasted from Charlie's rifle, that bullet just grazing Logan's arm. Sitting there in that corner, Logan knew he was a dead man if he didn't get off one accurate shot before the rifleman fired again. He had one advantage: the rifleman couldn't see him in the dark shadowy corner, but he could see the rifleman quite clearly. He pointed the revolver at arm's length and took as much time as he dared to fix his aim on the man on top of the coal. The slight rocking and bouncing of the train created more difficulty, but he knew this one had to count; he may not have another chance.

The discharge from the revolver rang out, and as if in slow motion, the rifleman doubled over, struggling to keep his stability. But then the train made a sudden lurch and the rifleman toppled first to his knees, and then went over the side of the car and out of sight. Logan wasn't certain if he had fallen, or purposely dove off into the darkness.

While all the shooting was going on, the frightened engineer and fireman climbed through the front locomotive cab windows onto the catwalks on each side of the boiler, leaving the unattended train speeding down the tracks.

Logan regained his ability to function well enough to maneuver to where he could see there was no one in the cab, but then he caught a glimpse of the engineer on the catwalk.

"Come back in the cab. Control this train," Logan called out. "The gunman made a quick exit."

The engineer had witnessed the end of the gun battle, and even though the shooting had stopped, he was apprehensive. Hold-up men usually worked in pairs. "Are there any more?" he called back to Logan.

"I don't think so. They'd be here by now. I think it's safe."

The engineer slowly and cautiously returned to the cab and resumed control of the runaway train, bringing it down to a crawling speed. The fireman returned into the cab as well. He rushed back to Logan in the tender.

"Should we stop and go back to find the body?" he asked, and then realized that Logan was severely wounded and bleeding badly.

"No, don't go back there!" Logan said. "There could be more waiting back there in the woods. And that's just what they would want you to do... stop."

"You're hurt pretty bad," the fireman said, helping Logan to a better sitting position. Then he yelled to the engineer. "Earl! Get this thing moving! The deputy's been shot! We need to get him to a doctor in Sparta right away!" Then he went back to shoveling coal to the firebox, and in a short while the train was rolling again, faster than usual.

Logan lay back. He didn't notice the discomfort of the lumpy coal. The pain in his shoulder was more intense than anything he had ever experienced.

Chapter 33

J ackson had completely lost track of the time. As he rode through Bangor and saw no train still at the depot, he felt in his pocket for his watch. It wasn't there; he realized in his haste getting dressed for supper that night, he had failed to pick it off the table by his bed. But it didn't matter. Regardless of the time, there was not a second to waste, and he urged Apollo to go on. Maybe they could catch the train stopped at the Rockland depot.

A few sprinkles of rain stung his face as Apollo raced on toward Rockland. It had been overcast all that day and night, but it had stayed dry and he hadn't seen any lightning or heard any thunder until now. Occasionally a lightning flash lit up the inky sky, but there didn't seem to be any threatening bolts reaching the ground, and he couldn't hear the faint thunder over Apollo's hooves beating the hardened earth on the road beneath him.

The train had already left the Rockland station. No sign of people lingering or milling around in the depot meant that nothing out of the ordinary with the eastbound train had been noticed, and it also meant that the robbery at Miller's Crossing was already in progress. Jackson slapped Apollo on the rump with his hat. "Come on, Apollo! I know you're probably tired, but we have to try to help Logan."

Apollo rose to the need and galloped off to the east. Light rain fell steadily now, but it didn't concern Jackson, and it certainly didn't seem to hinder Apollo's performance.

He slowed Apollo to just a trot when they neared the edge of the wooded area and approached the spot he recognized as Miller's Crossing. It was where the road crossed the tracks, and was the very spot where he and Charlie had camped one night to watch the trains and to lay the plans for a hold-up.

There was no train there now. He was too late. He stopped Apollo at the crossing and dismounted. In the lightning flashes he could see the entire vicinity, and he dreaded to find what his mind was expecting to see. But he saw no bodies lying in the muddy roadway, or in the ditches along the tracks. If the gang had been there, the rain had already washed away any tracks or signs of struggle.

Jackson didn't know that the notes from Charlie had never been delivered to the rest of the gang members, and he didn't know the robbery had never occurred. All he knew was what Charlie had told him, and that Charlie had boarded that train with the intentions of carrying out the plans, and with the confidence that the others would be waiting for him at Miller's Crossing. And he knew that Logan was on that train, and that was the most disturbing thought of all. He sensed that something bad had happened, and even with his efforts to prevent it, he had failed. There was nothing more he could do now.

He swung himself into the saddle and rode toward Sparta.

Chapter 34

"**W**hy is the train stopping in Sparta?" the sheriff asked in a disgusted tone. "I told the conductor not to stop until—"

"The eastbound train is already here," Clarence Thorbus said peering out the window and pointing to the siding at the opposite side of the depot. A small crowd of people were gathered, flanking the locomotive and coal tender. A horse and buggy raced away toward town.

Colby bolted from his seat to the coach door, and all the deputies followed. They didn't wait for the conductor or the porters. They were jumping from the coach even before the train had come to a complete stop.

"What's goin' on here?" the sheriff yelled as he approached the eastbound locomotive, smoke still pouring from its stack and steam hissing from under the engine.

The gathering turned and saw the sheriff and his men rapidly coming toward them. They parted to expose the engineer and fireman standing on the ground at the rear of the locomotive, both appearing a bit shaken.

"Mr. Benjamin from the livery was here with a buggy to pick up someone getting off the westbound," one of the onlookers offered. "But he just left with your deputy, heading for the hospital. He was shot and bleeding pretty bad."

"What deputy?" Colby barked. "All my deputies are with me."

"Not Logan," said Clarence. "Remember? You sent him to La Crosse today."

Colby stopped dead in his tracks with a startled expression, as if he had encountered a brick wall. He had tried to keep Logan away from the trouble, and now it occurred to him that he had put him right in the middle of it. He gathered his wits again and pulled his hat brim down to better protect his eyes from the rain. He turned to the engineer and fireman. "I'm Sheriff Colby. What happened?" he snarled.

"W-well, Sheriff," the fireman said. "Thanks to your deputy, this train didn't get robbed."

"Yeah," the engineer chimed in. "He told us that there was a whole gang waitin' fer us, and that we shouldn't stop."

"Well, how did he get shot?" Colby asked.

"One of the robbers was already on the train, hidin' on the roof, I guess," the fireman went on.

"Charlie McCoy," Colby mumbled, recalling the telegram he received from Jackson Evans.

"He tried ambushin' me 'n Earl, but I reckon he didn't see Deputy Logan in the coal tender... prob'ly too dark."

"What was Logan doing in the coal tender?"

"Said he had to get off the train in Sparta without bein' seen. Said he could do that from the tender."

"You still didn't tell me how Logan got shot."

"Well, when me 'n Earl heard someone shout that we should throw up our hands, we turned 'round 'n saw him standin' there on top of the coal, 'n he was pointin' a pretty big gun at us. Next thing we know, there's lead flyin' back 'n forth between the guy on top of the coal and Deputy Logan. The deputy must've caught one just before he drilled one into the man with the rifle. He fell over the side."

"So... how's Logan?"

"Hit real bad... bleeding a lot. He was unconscious by the time we got here... maybe dead."

Colby turned to his deputies, all standing behind him and listening to the report from the train men. "Go talk to everybody on this train... find out if they saw anything, and make sure there ain't any more of the gang still on the train."

The deputies all headed for the passenger coaches. Colby grabbed Clarence's sleeve. "Clarence, wait," Colby said. "You come with me. We're going to the hospital."

Poor planning had left all the sheriff's horses at Tunnel City, and there were no more available at this late hour around the depot. Colby turned up his collar and adjusted his hat as he stood just inside the depot doorway with Clarence, looking out at the dismal night. "C'mon, Clarence," he said. "We'll have to walk."

They had been gone for twenty minutes when a lone rider appeared out of the darkness from the west. The eastbound train had pulled out just minutes earlier, and all the deputies were gathered along the tracks where the train had been. Deputy George Clark noticed the rider as he passed beneath a street lamp at the end of the depot building. He studied the horse and rider for a few moments as the rider dismounted and tied the reins to a hitching rail. He nudged Deputy Sam Gorman. "Isn't that one of Logan's horses?"

Sam turned. "Sure looks like Apollo to me."

Jackson noticed the group of men by the tracks, and he caught a glimpse of sparkles of light reflecting on their badges. He watched as two of the men came toward him. There was no point in trying to run from them; he was on their side now, and he hoped they knew it. But they didn't look as though they were coming over to invite him to an ice cream social.

"Yep," Sam Gorman said. "This here's definitely Apollo."

"Thought so," said George Clark. "Looks like we caught us a horse thief, Sam."

"But I didn't steal him," Jackson protested. "I just borrowed him. Honest!"

"Sure you did," George sneered. "You *borrowed* Apollo right out of Logan's barn. And you're one of the train robbery gang, too." He drew his revolver and aimed it at Jackson. "Now we're gonna take you on over to the jailhouse."

Jackson had been wondering how far behind Mr. Logan was, but now he didn't have to wonder. Mr. Logan quietly stepped from the shadows right behind the two deputies. They heard the click as he cocked the hammer of his hunting rifle.

"He's telling you the truth," Mr. Logan said. "And you'd better put that pistol away before I put a slug in your right leg."

George and Sam both recognized his voice and slowly turned toward Mr. Logan.

"Are you gonna put that thing away?" Mr. Logan asked. "Or do I have to shoot you both? I will, y' know."

George cautiously holstered his gun. Sam stared at Mr. Logan with unblinking owl eyes.

"That's better," Mr. Logan said, and pointed his rifle at the ground. "You two should be ashamed of yourselves. Hans has told me all about this. Jackson, here, is trying to help you, and you don't have the good sense to listen to him."

"But Otis... we thought—"

"Well, you thought wrong," Mr. Logan growled. "Now, where's my boy? And where's the sheriff? I want a word with him."

"Otis," George said. "Hans was shot tonight by one of the robbery gang. Benjamin hauled him to the hospital in a carriage. The sheriff and Clarence Thorbus went over there a while ago."

"Thorbus!" Mr. Logan said. "Well, at least there's someone among you with a little sense." He turned to Jackson who was about ready to break down in tears. "C'mon, Jackson. Mount up. We're going to the hospital."

"Otis!" George said. "We'll ride with you."

Mr. Logan stared down at George from his saddle. "No you won't." Then he watched Jackson mount Apollo. "You ready, Jackson?"

"Yes, sir."

In a moment they were gone.

Chapter 35

"How did you know where to find me?" Jackson asked Otis Logan as they rode up Water Street.

"That was easy," Otis replied. "You said Hans was on the train from La Crosse, and when I didn't see anything at Miller's Crossing, the next stop for that train is Sparta."

"Yeah, I guess that would be easy to figure out. Well, I'm glad you showed up when you did."

Jackson was actually making small talk just to keep him from thinking about what might have happened to Logan. Otis Logan recognized the boy's worry. "Don't blame yourself," he said. "We don't even know what's happened to Hans. I'm sure he'll be fine."

Jackson knew Mr. Logan was worried about his son, too, and he was just trying to be optimistic. But Jackson couldn't rid his mind of guilt. Everything that had happened was because of him. If he hadn't said anything to Logan, none of this would have occurred. The robbery probably would have gone as planned, and no lawmen would have been there, and Logan would be investigating the incident instead of being one of its casualties.

The lights shone brightly from the windows of the lower level of the hospital house. Sheriff Colby and Deputy Thorbus met Jackson and Otis just inside the front door. Their expressions were grim, and before the sheriff spoke a single word, Jackson's eyes were wet with tears again.

"Otis," the sheriff said. "I'm sorry this had to happen this way. I sent Hans off to La Crosse today to keep him away from a dangerous situation."

Otis Logan remained silent. His tall, confident stature seemed to droop a little. His nervous hands fidgeted with his hat he was now holding.

"But that was before we knew the train robbery plans had changed," Colby continued. "If we had only known—"

Otis was already tired of the sheriff's drivel and he couldn't hold back the question any longer. "Is Hans dead?"

Jackson held his breath, his entire body rigid in anticipation of bad news.

"Oh, no," the sheriff said. "He took a bullet in the shoulder and Doc Sarles is taking care of him. I talked to Hans just before you got here. He's gonna be okay."

Mr. Logan's mouth curled into a little smile and he looked at Jackson. "You hear that, Jackson? He's gonna be okay."

Jackson wiped away the tears from his cheek with the back of his hand. "Yeah, I heard," he said as a smile came to his face, too.

The sheriff stared at the boy. "Are you Jackson Evans?"

"Yes, sir."

"Well," Colby said. He stepped directly in front of Jackson. "You're one of the robbery gang. I'll have to place you under arrest and hold you in the jail."

Otis Logan stepped between them, towering a head taller than the sheriff. "Over my dead body!" he said, glaring at Colby. "This boy is the only reason the train *didn't* get robbed. Hans has told me the whole story. You lay one finger on this boy and you'll answer to me ... understand?"

Colby backed away. He'd known Otis for a long time, and he knew Otis to be a man of honor and integrity. And right now, he knew Otis meant exactly what he said. "W-well... I suppose... for you... I guess I could reconsider..."

Mr. Logan continued to stare Colby in the eyes. "Good," he said in a stern tone. "And I trust Clarence Thorbus, here, to be an honest witness to all this." Then he made eye contact with Clarence.

Clarence smiled and nodded.

Just then Doctor Sarles came from another room, blood stains spattered on his white shirt. He was wiping his hands with a towel. "Hello, Otis," he said. "Good news... Hans will be okay. I got the bullet out. Hans is young and strong, and I'm sure he'll recover quite nicely. But he needs some rest right now. He can stay here overnight."

"Okay, Doc," Sheriff Colby said. Then he turned to Otis and offered his hand. "Me and Clarence will be going now. Hans told us where to find the body of the robber who shot him, so we'll just be on our way." He nodded to Clarence and then they left.

Body? Jackson thought. He hadn't heard the part about Logan returning the gunfire, or any of the talk of a body. He quickly began adding together the few facts he did know: Charlie McCoy was aboard that train the last he saw him; Logan had been shot by one of the gang members... on that train; nothing he had seen at the depot indicated that Charlie was in custody. Could it be that Charlie was the body the sheriff had referred to?

"Can we talk to Hans?" Mr. Logan asked the doctor when the sheriff and Clarence were gone.

"Sure," Doctor Sarles said. "The nurse is getting him into a bed down the hall right now." He motioned for them to follow as he started toward the corridor.

Shaky and weakened from the loss of blood, Logan sat on the edge of a white-sheeted bed. A middle aged woman in a black and white dress swabbed his face and his one good arm with a wet towel. He was still smudged with coal dust and his blue jeans that lay in a heap on the floor were nearly black. His left shoulder and arm were wrapped in white bandages, a little red spot still showing where the blood had soaked through. When the nurse had finished, she gently pushed him back onto the pillow, lifted his legs onto the bed, and partially covered him with a sheet.

Logan noticed the doctor walk into the room, and right behind him, Logan's father. "Pop!" he said, barely audible.

Mr. Logan rushed to the bedside and put his hand on his son's good arm. "I'm so glad you're okay, son," he said. "You don't know how worried I was there for a little while. And I want you to know that I'm mighty proud of what you did."

"Thanks Pop." Logan's voice was weak, hardly more than a whisper. "But I think it was more luck than anything."

"That's okay, son. We won't tell anybody." Otis winked.

Jackson had been outside the door. He didn't know what to say to Logan, but he desperately wanted to see him.

"There's somebody else here to see you, too," Mr. Logan told his son, and then he turned to the open door. "Hey, you! Out there in the hall. Come in here!"

Jackson poked his head around the corner, and then cautiously stepped into the room. When he saw Logan smiling at him, his reluctance faded and he hustled to the bed beside Mr. Logan. He silently stared at Logan's bare torso and the bandages on his shoulder. He still didn't know what to say.

"Doc says I'm gonna be okay," Logan said, seeing that his

friend was truly concerned. "Just a little gunshot wound."

"I—I'm sorry, Logan, for gettin' you into this."

"Don't be sorry, Jackson. And I'm glad to see you're okay."

"Well, if it hadn't been for your father, I might not be here."

Dr. Sarles saw that Logan was in pain, and that even talking was putting a great deal of strain on him. "I think it would be a good idea if we let Hans rest now," he said.

"I'll bring you some clean clothes tomorrow," Otis said. He caressed Logan's good arm and then put a hand on Jackson's shoulder. "Okay, Jackson. Let's go home. We'll come back in the morning."

Jackson squeezed out a worried smile and they went out of the room.

Chapter 36

"Benjamin! We need some horses and a wagon," the sheriff demanded of the livery stable man. "We're going out to pick up a body by the railroad tracks."

"Just a team and wagon?"

"No... we'll need three saddle horses, too. I'll take Argo and two others."

"Oh, I can't let you take Argo," Benjamin objected.

"Why not?"

"I promised Logan."

Colby decided he'd had enough confrontation with Otis. "All right... then *three others*. We'll be waiting at the depot."

The rain had stopped by the time Benjamin brought the team and wagon with three saddled riding horses tied behind. Colby, Clark, and Gorman mounted the saddled horses, and Clarence took the reins of the team with the other special deputies and several lanterns in the wagon. They headed west on the wagon road to begin their search at Miller's Crossing.

Two hours later they returned with nothing more than a muddy red silk bandana and a rain-soaked gray felt hat.

"Go home and get some sleep. We'll continue the search tomorrow in daylight," the sheriff announced to his men. "Sam and George can go over to Tunnel City and bring back all our horses."

News traveled rapidly through the town when sunshine finally returned the next morning. Deputy Hans Logan had shot and killed the notorious outlaw from the wild west, Tom Nixon, who had disappeared years ago, and who the Pinkerton Agency had all but given up trying to find. Single-handedly, Hans Logan risked his life and had deterred Nixon's gang from robbing the train. The whole town hummed with the great news, and there was already talk of voting Hans Logan into the Sheriff's Office.

It was great news, and the newspaper reporters were anticipating their stories that would celebrate Hans Logan's heroic deed. Unfortunately, it wasn't all true.

While the sheriff waited for his deputies to return from Tunnel City with all the horses, he went to the hospital to have another talk with Logan. When he arrived, he quickly learned that the several newspaper reporters who had gathered around Hans, Otis, and Jackson in the entrance lobby were more interested in Logan than they could possibly be about anything the sheriff had to say. They all saw him enter, but they returned to focus their attention on Logan.

"It's only because of my good friend, Jackson Evans, that the westbound train wasn't robbed of the logging company's payroll last night." He put his uninjured arm around Jackson's shoulders. Jackson's face turned red. "If it was Tom Nixon on the train," he continued, "I only know that one of the shots I fired hit him, and he fell off the train."

"But you didn't kill him," the sheriff broke in. "We went out to bring back the body last night, but we only found this." He held up the red bandana. "Apparently," Colby said, now addressing the reporters, "Logan only wounded Nixon. Me and my men will start hunting him down in about an hour."

"You won't find him," Jackson said, eyeing the red handkerchief, the corners still knotted together and folded to form a face mask.

The reporters turned their attention from the sheriff to Jackson. "Why not?" one of them asked.

"I worked with Charlie—Tom Nixon—all winter. He was clever enough to escape the Pinkerton's search eight years ago, and he's probably long gone from here, too. He knows how to cover his tracks."

"You knew Tom Nixon?"

"Yeah, but like I said, the sheriff will be wasting his time looking for him. Who he should be after is Joshua Avery. He's the leader of the gang, and he was the one who wanted to rob the logging company payroll from the westbound train."

All eyes were on Colby. "Sheriff," one of the reporters said. "Seems like these two boys know more about all this than you do. Are you going after Joshua Avery?"

Red faced, the sheriff responded. "Of course I'm going after Avery... and all the rest of the gang members, as well."

Logan and Jackson backed away now that the reporters were firing a barrage of intimidating questions at the sheriff. "Will you get Argo from Benjamin's livery stable?" Logan asked.

"Already done," Jackson said. "Your dad and I went over there this morning before we came here. He's right outside waiting for you. Sure you can ride?"

Logan nodded. "Let's go home."

Epilog

Later that day, Joshua Avery and Louis Reed were caught at the West Salem depot, about to board the eastbound *Chicago & North Western* with one way tickets to Chicago. They were jailed and held for trial.

John Schultz, Max Jensen, and Eddy Slokum were all arrested a few days later, but because they had not actually taken part in the holdup, they were released.

The rifle recovered from the coal tender used in the attempted holdup had been a gun from Joshua Avery's rack at the saloon. And Jackson Evans' testimony at the trial strongly persuaded the jury to find Avery guilty. He was sentenced to twenty years in a Federal prison.

Louis Reed was released because there lack of evidence against him. But bad publicity doomed his livery business, and he soon left town.

Hans Logan recovered from his injuries and returned to duty, but only for a short time. Although he was regarded highly in the public eye and among county officials, this close encounter with deadly circumstances had been enough, and he ended his law enforcement career. He entered college at

Madison, and became a veterinarian.

Jackson Evans returned to his home in La Crosse. He took a stronger interest in the mighty Mississippi River that he had always loved. He hired on as a deckhand on one of McDonald's log rafting steamboats, and eventually earned the position as First Mate.

Charlie McCoy—Tom Nixon—covered his tracks. He was never seen again.

ABOUT THE AUTHOR

Born into a farm family in the late 1940s, J.L. Fredrick lived his youth in rural Western Wisconsin, a modest but comfortable life not far from the Mississippi River. His father was a farmer, and his mother, an elementary school teacher. He attended a one-room country school for his first seven years of education.

Wisconsin has been home all his life, with exception of a few years in Minnesota and Florida. After college in La Crosse, Wisconsin and a stint with Uncle Sam during the Viet Nam era, the next few years were unsettled as he explored and experimented with life's options. He entered into the transportation industry in 1975.

Since 2001 he has eight published novels to his credit, and one history volume, *Rivers, Roads, & Rails,* a non-fiction account of Midwestern history that focuses on the development of transportation during the pioneer days— steamboats, stagecoaches, and the beginnings of the Midwest's railroads—and the impact they had on the growth and prosperity of Midwest communities. He was a featured author during Grand Excursion 2004.

J.L. Fredrick currently resides at Madison, Wisconsin.

www.ingramcontent.com/pod-product-compliance
Lightning Source LLC
Chambersburg PA
CBHW051958220626
47052CB00004B/999